Darbi

His Ladies with the Lamps
Book 3

By

Ronna M. Bacon

The Ladies with the Lamps

Matthew 25: 6-10

6 "And at midnight a cry was heard: 'Behold, the bridegroom is coming; go out to meet him!' 7 Then all those virgins arose and trimmed their lamps. 8 And the foolish said to the wise, 'Give us some of your oil, for our lamps are going out.' 9 But the wise answered, saying, 'No, lest there should not be enough for us and you; but go rather to those who sell, and buy for yourselves.' 10 And while they went to buy, the bridegroom came, and those who were ready went in with him to the wedding; and the door was shut.

Darbi

Psalms 118:6

The Lord is on my side; I will not fear. What can man do to me?

Psalms 91:4

He shall cover you with His feathers, and under His wings you shall take refuge; His truth shall be your shield and buckler.

NKJV

Table of Contents

Shrugging deeper into his jacket again the cold of the day, Flynn Carson strode rapidly through the forests that bordered his home. He had returned to his town after a number of years, glad to be home. But the phone call that he was on? It was disturbing. His phone had chimed just ten minutes earlier. When he answered it, he could hear rustling but no voice. His repeated helloes had elicited a response. Just as he was about to set it aside, he heard some soft muttering and a female voice. Flynn had frowned at that, not sure who would be calling. The only ladies with his number was his aunt.

His eyes in rapid movement Flynn listened to the muttering, hearing the words asking for help, and then the comment of what did she just do. And just what did the man with her want from her? She didn't know him and had nothing that he wanted from her.

Flynn sighed, knowing that the number was not one he recognized. He didn't need this. Coming home from a western province to his home town had not been easy. There were things here that he did not want to face, but God seemed to have other plans. His work as a journalist was been the main focus of his life until the accident that had laid him up with a broken leg for months. He had healed but his heart was no longer in his work. That troubled him to no end.

Pausing for a moment, still hidden by the tree and brush, Flynn's eyes searched the small clearing.

They paused on the man standing there. No, he decided, he didn't know him. He watched as the man paced, not leaving the clearing. Flynn dropped his gaze, pausing once more in his forward walk. There was a lady on the ground, her arm across her face. He could hear the soft sobs from where he stood. Anger raced through him and he made a move to walk forward, only to stop.

The man, a heavyset man at that, stood over the woman, his words inaudible to Flynn. The woman slumped down further to the ground, her hands around her head to protect herself. Flynn searched the area, not seeing anyone else, before he charged forward. His sudden attack took the man by surprise as Flynn launched himself at the man, a swift blow from his fist ending the fight before it even began.

Turning then from the man, Flynn simply gathered the woman, no lady, he thought, into his arms and turning, ran for the path and his home. He didn't hear a sound of the man coming after him. He prayed that he could get the lady to safety and then to help.

Shoving the back door shut with his foot, Flynn reached awkwardly to lock the door. A chair was pulled out with his foot and he carefully set his burden on it. The lady didn't look up. Flynn sighed. He wasn't any good with ladies in trouble. He never had been. Reaching for a bottle of water, he wrapped her hand around it and then crouched beside her.

The lady raised her head, fear, no terror, on her face and in her eyes. She stared at Flynn, not recognizing him, but somehow knowing that he had saved her.

"I'm sorry. I'll leave." The lady, Darbi Whitman by name, made a move to stand, Flynn's hand on her arm keeping her in place.

"No, he's still out there. Here. Have some water." Flynn was on his feet, a drawer opened and a cloth retrieved. He simply rinsed it out in as warm a water as he could and then handed it to her. Darbi refused to take it, her eyes on Flynn, a frown on her face.

Flynn sighed. He reached to gently wipe the dirt and tears from her face, finding her leaning into his touch. That puzzled him and it showed on his face.

"You're safe. I don't know who that was, but you're safe with me. I'm Flynn Carson. This is my hometown and I've just returned to it."

Darbi studied him, not sure about him before she felt the nudge from God that she always felt when she met new people. She wasn't great at that, she knew.

"I'm Darbi Whitman. Thank you." Her voice was low and still tear-filled.

"What was that all about?" Flynn shifted on his chair to stare at his back door. "He was on my property. I didn't recognize him. Do you know him?"

Darbi shook her head, regretting it as a headache pounded behind her eyes for a moment.

"No, I don't. I had simply gone out to get a newspaper and a coffee and was back at home. Yes, I was walking. He appeared in my home, forced me to go with him, and I couldn't get away.. He wouldn't let me." Darbi frowned at Flynn. "I don't know him. He asked for something. But it isn't making sense what he has asked for."

"What was that?"

"Jewelry. Gems. I don't have that. Why would he ask that?" Darbi's face showed her puzzlement. "Do you know him?"

Flynn shook his head, on his feet to make tea for them. At least, he hoped that she drank tea. He didn't have coffee in his house at the moment but he knew himself well enough that if she drank coffee as she stated that would be a part of his grocery shopping.

"I'm sorry. I'll leave." Darbi was on her feet, moving towards the door.

Flynn sighed, simply reaching out to stop her. She flinched under his hand and he frowned at her. He shoved her down into a chair and crouched beside her, seeing the fear on her face.

"I need to call someone for you or take you home to your place." He watched as she finally nodded. "I'm sorry. I don't have coffee right now but will tea do?"

"Tea?" Darbi shrugged, not sure what was happening. She looked past him as the back door violently flew open and screamed.

Flynn didn't have a chance to rise, the blow to his back sending him to the floor. He grimace with pain, the words spewed at him not audible through the pain. Hauled to his feet, he was forced from the room, his feet stumbling over one another before he was shoved once more towards the path to the clearing. He could vaguely hear Darbi's protests and sobs. Flynn knew that he needed to keep his wits about him. Only that didn't seem possible at the moment.

Darbi struggled to escape the hand that gripped her arm. She just couldn't. She was forced to walk back along the path to the clearing, her eyes on Flynn. She prayed that he was okay but knew that he was hurting. The pair were forced through the clearing and into the woods on the other side. Darbi's breath caught in her throat. She knew where this was heading and she had no desire to end up there.

God, where are You? I know that You are here but we need to get away. I don't know that we can. My new friend is hurt because of me. Please, dear Lord? Let him get away. It doesn't matter about me.

Chapter 2

Flynn swayed on his feet as he was pulled to a stop, his head pounding from the blows that he had been given as he walked. His eyes closed as he fought the nausea welling inside him. He felt an arm come around him and a body leaning on him. *It had to be Darbi,* he thought. *Lord, I have no idea who this is or why. Protect us. Free us. Help me to help this lady who I would like to count on as a friend.*

Darbi had watched with horror as Flynn had stumbled along ahead of her. She tried to wrench her arm free to race to help him. That had not been possible. The man who had originally held her captive had too tight a grip on her. It was just impossible for her to escape. When she was released at last, she ran for Flynn, an arm around him. Only, she knew that if he fell, she would too. And she would not be able to bring him back to his feet. That was obvious. He was just too tall. *What is it,* she wondered, *with all these tall guys in our lives? First Brinn with her Gareth. And then Chani with her Ronan.* Even her father and uncle had been tall. She sniffed, suddenly missing the protection that her father always provided. To find out that her parents and uncle and aunt had been murdered had devastated her sister, Brinn, and her cousins, Chani and Eilis. And her Aunt Ashlynn? Losing her brothers and then becoming guardian to four girls when she was just starting her life? That had not been fair, but her aunt had not shown that at all

Her dark brown hair flying around her face and her dark brown eyes shadowed with fear, Darbi wrapped her arm around Flynn. She sought for a way to escape, not seeing one. She had no idea who he really was. All she knew was that he had come to her rescue and that she felt safe with him. Only, they weren't so safe anymore. Not while they were in these men's hands. Darbie had no idea what they wanted and that terrified her.

Flynn's arm came around Darbi and pulled her tight to him. He blinked rapidly, his eyes clearing at last. He watched the men closely, not sure what was happening. His deep blue eyes dropped to the lady holding on to him. He frowned. He didn't hold ladies like this. Only it seemed that he was. Flynn looked around, ready to run. The breeze tossed his blond curls, causing him to raise a hand to brush them from his face.

Darbi was scared, she had to admit. This was well above what she had ever experienced. Her sister, Brinn, and her cousin, Chani, had and had barely survived their adventures as they termed them.

Forced to the ground, Flynn kept his arm around Darbi, holding her tight to him. He was ready to rise and flee if the chance came. Only that didn't seem to be happening. Just what they were waiting for, he wasn't sure. But someone else was expected. That person was an unknown and he really didn't want that to happen. He sighed to himself. Why had he ever returned here?

Darbi shifted her weight, the cold of the ground seeping into her flesh. She couldn't stay there long on the ground, she knew. She too watched the men, not sure what to expect either. She had begged God that He would spare her this type of adventure. But it seemed that He had other plans. Those plans He had not shared as yet. She prayed that He did soon.

Ashlyn Whitman turned from the door of the duplex where Darbi lived. They had planned to meet for lunch. Only Darbi was not answering her door. Her car was there. She was always reluctant to use her key to her nieces' places but this was one time it was warranted.

Walking through the house, Ashlynn frowned. There was no sign of Darbi, who would not have been away if she knew a family member was coming. She frowned as she stood in the kitchen. This was not the way that Darbi left it. A mug lay on the floor, a full cup of coffee spilled there. A chair was on its side.

Ashlynn drew in a deep breath. Darbi was missing. Where was she? Retreating to her car, Ashlynn reached for her phone, making the call that she prayed that she would never have to make. Not for one of her girls.

Turning as she heard a vehicle, Ashlyn walked towards the officer. She was more and more worried as Darbi had not appeared.

"Ashlynn?" Jackson Troy frowned at her. He was familiar with Ashlynn and the four girls from church. "You're here? What's going on? Where's Darbi?"

"I don't know. We were to meet today for a meal. She didn't answer the door. When I went in, I looked for her. There is a mug of coffee on the floor and a chair overturned. She is not there at all."

Jackson gave her a keen look and nodded. The officers had talked among themselves. They had all fully expected another one of the Whitman ladies to face danger. They just had not been sure which one of the three would.

"Stay put. I'll look around. She doesn't have any animals?"

"A gray tabby cat. I didn't see her, but she hides if someone comes in. She always has."

"Okay. I'll keep my eye out for her. Head back for your car and stay warm."

Jackson walked through the house, puzzled. There was just no sign of Darbi. Other than the mug of coffee spilt on the floor, there was nothing to show that she had been there that day.

Ashlynn watched as another patrol vehicle pulled up and the officer headed for Jackson. They spoke for a while before that officer headed for the neighbours.

This is not good, Ashlyn muttered to herself. *Darbi really isn't there. Where is she, Lord? Protect her wherever that is. Help her to come home safe and sound. I don't know that we can go through another adventure like the other two girls. But You are in control. You know best.*

Frank, an investigator with the force but also a good friend of Ashlynn, shut his vehicle door quietly. His eyes were on Ashlynn before he walked towards her. He noticed that she jumped as he stopped beside her.

"Frank? You're here? I didn't think that you would be." Ashlynn breathed a prayer of thankfulness that he was.

"I caught the call and came. You knew that I would, Ashlynn. If it involves you and the girls, then I'm here. I spoke with my supervisor. He agreed. Now, what happened?"

"What happened?" Frank grinned as her voice rose. "I come for a meal with Darbi. Only she's not here. I have no idea where she is. Do you?"

Frank shook his head, his grin still in place.

"No, I'm sorry. I don't, Ashlynn. Hang tight while I see what's happening." Frank walked away, leaving Ashlynn staring at him and then at the house.

Her phone chiming caught at her attention and she pulled it out. Brinn! Just what was needed, now wasn't it?

"Aunt Ash? Have you seen Darbi? I've been trying to call her and it goes straight to voice mail. Her texts are not answered either." Brinn's voice was rushed, not like her at all.

"I haven't. I'm at her place now, Brinn. Only she's not here." Ashlynn moved her phone away from her ear at the scream that Brinn gave. "Brinn? We don't know where she is. The police are here now as well as Frank. They're looking for her."

"She's gone and done what we did. She wasn't supposed to." Brinn was torn. She wanted to be at her sister's, only she was walking one of her client's dog and couldn't leave. "Call me if you find her or you hear anything?"

"I will, Brinn. Just pray for her." Ashlynn slumped against her car, her eyes on the house, not seeing her niece running towards her as she normally would.

Chapter 3

Brinn ran towards her aunt's home that evening, her husband at her side, as she dodged the following now. Gareth was worried about his sister-in-law but also about his wife. This was not what she needed, he knew, but God had allowed it. They had to trust Him, no matter what happened.

Shaking off the snow, Brinn removed her jacket and dropped it on the hall rack. She then searched for her aunt and cousins, finding them in Ashlynn's office. Chani's boyfriend, Ronan, was just returning with a tray of coffee and tea for them.

"Aunt Ash? Any word?" Brinn rushed towards her aunt, finding her arms folding around her.

"No, not yet. Frank is working on it, but he said they really couldn't tell what happened. It looks as if she went missing this morning."

"She had to work. No, she didn't. The office was closed today, wasn't it?" Brinn was muttering to herself, trying to figure it all out. Gareth simply wrapped her into his arms when Ashlynn released her.

"They were, Brinn." Ashlynn watched her closely, worried about her.

"Where is she? Does anyone know?" Chani was on her feet, reaching for her cousin before Eilis moved in to hug both ladies.

"We don't know. Her security camera was destroyed during the night. Frank pulled it up on her laptop. She had given him that data when you went through what you did, Brinn. He said he couldn't see anyone around it.'

"He would have seen someone." Ronan reached for Chani, drawing her down to the couch, his arm wrapped around her as he sat with her. Eilis perched beside her, her face white with worry.

"Has she said anything about anyone? Did she have trouble with anyone?" Eilis was grabbing at straws, knowing what the answer was, she thought.

"Not that I know off. But she has been withdrawn to some extent the last couple of weeks." Brinn sighed, rubbing at her temple. "I asked her about it but she just shrugged it off. She hasn't said anything at all."

"And she won't. Not unless she was sure of her facts. If it was just a feeling, then she wouldn't." Ashlynn was on her feet, heading for the door, opening it to find Frank standing there. "Frank? Peg? You two are here?"

"We are, Ashlynn. As friends. We just wanted to meet with you all and cover you with prayer. This is puzzling for sure." Frank walked towards the office where he heard the voices.

Peg watched him and then turned to Ashlynn, studying her friend of many years.

"Ashlynn? What can you tell us?"

"Not a lot." Ashlynn drew in a deep breath, her eyes on the picture of a lighthouse hanging on an entryway wall. "She hasn't said anything if something was going on, but that's her."

"It is her. I just wish it hadn't happened. Did you call the pastor?" Peg wrapped an arm around her friend and turned her to the kitchen, shoving her down into a chair before she sat as well.

"I did. This morning. Or at least I tried. I could only leave a voice message." Ashlynn sighed as her phone chimed. "It's been doing that a lot today, with no one there."

Peg shared a look with Frank who had come to find the ladies.

"Ashlynn? Do you know the number that's calling?" Frank's voice caused Ashlynn to jump, her eyes on him and then on her young nieces.

"No, I don't. When I answer, they hang up. Is it Darbi?"

Frank shrugged, not sure how to reply.

"I don't know, Ashlynn. If it was, she would say something. May I take a look at the number?" Frank took the phone as Ashlynn nodded, his eyes on her before they dropped to the phone. He froze, knowing the number. Someone was trying to reach out to Ashlynn but they were trying to cover their tracks as well. They knew that Ashlynn would go to Frank at some point. "Excuse me, ladies, Ronan, Gareth. I need to take a look at this." Frank was away, his jacket on, as he headed for his vehicle.

"Toad? This is Frank." Frank wasted no time in returning the call. It was an undercover officer, he knew.

"Frank? Thank God. I was hoping Ashlynn reached out to you. What's going on with her?"

"Darbi."

"Darbi? Then what I heard is true. She's missing. And so is Flynn Carson."

"Flynn? I didn't know that he had come back to town."

"He's been back for a couple of weeks. Staying very low key and close to home. He went through some stuff a while ago. That's why he came home."

"I see. I take it that you have spoken with him."

"I have. I can't say what is going on now. Rumours are just that. Rumours. You'll need to send someone out to his place."

"And where would that be?" Frank reached for a pad of paper, his pen poised to write down the address.

"His parents. They left it to him. I think that's part of why he came home. Only it's isolated and would be a good place to hide someone."

"It would. I've been there a few times." Frank chewed at his lip, knowing that he needed to act on the tip but not quite sure how to.

"I've been out there, Frank. I can see where there are a lot of prints, heading into the woods. If they're out there, we need to find them." Toad was worried, that was a given. Darbi had been kind to him over the years, not realizing that he was an officer. He wanted to repay her and her family in some way.

"I know. Let me head out there. Peg is here with Ashlynn and can stay." Frank drove off, not seeing Ronan and Gareth standing on the porch, watching him and waiting for him to come back.

"Where's he off to?" Gareth was puzzled, to say the least.

"He likely got called away." Ronan stared out into the night, seeing that the snow had slowed. "I just pray that she is under shelter somewhere."

"Me too." Gareth turned for the house, his hand hesitating on the door latch before he shoved the door open, Ronan following him.

Chapter 4

Darbi stirred late that night. She looked around, rubbing at her eyes, not sure where she was. All she knew was that she was not at home and someone was holding her tight. She grew afraid, trying to push herself away from the man but unable to move away. Darbi's head twisted as she tried to see him but was unable to in the dark. She had no idea where she was.

Flynn roused as he felt Darbi stirring, not sure either where he was. He looked around, not seeing much in the darkness. All he knew was that they were somewhere in a building. And that he held a beautiful lady in his arms. He withdrew his arms and stood, heading for the door that he could barely see. He touched it, finding it swinging open under his finger tips.

Darbi had watched, on her feet, fear still flowing through her mind. Something in her heart was telling her that she could trust this man, this Flynn. Only, she didn't know that she really could.

Flynn turned, a hand reaching for Darbi. She stared at it and then up at him. Finally, she reached for it, finding his grasp tight and strong.

"Can we leave?" Darbi didn't dare speak very loud. She was afraid that the men were still there.

"I think so." Flynn pushed the door open all the way, hesitating to step through. His head tilted as he listened, not hearing anything. He stepped outside, Darbi's hand clutching at the back of his jacket. He

———

looked around and then up, finding the snow that had started slowing in its fall. Flynn knew where they were and just how long it would take to walk back to his home. That was not a walk which he was looking forward to. He didn't know how Darbi would fare.

"Where are we?" Darbi's voice was barely above a whisper.

"Near my home. We can walk to it, but it will take a bit. Are you up to it?"

Darbi snorted, surprising him.

"It's not like we have any choice, now does it? I don't see any vehicle waiting for us."

Flynn pulled on his gloves, reaching for her hand

"What's with this, Flynn? I don't hold hands with men." Darbi refused to take his hand.

"I didn't think that you did. Right now? You need to. We have some rough terrain to go through, it's night, and it's been snowing. So enough already." He simply reached for her hand, holding it tight as she struggled to take it back.

Darbi finally gave up the battle. She was cold, tired, hungry, and thirsty. Allowing him to do this? It just might get her home sooner. She followed him, the cold seeping through her jacket. Darbi had not really dressed for the cold that had fallen. Not when she had been forced from her home that morning. She had been allowed to grab her boots, a jacket, hat, and mitts but that was all.

Flynn could feel Darbi's steps starting to lag and he sighed. He looked around to find a place for her to sit for a moment. Wiping the snow off of a tree stump, he waited as she sat. He crouched down beside her, his head moving constantly as he kept watch.

"Flynn? Are you okay?" Darbi winced as her voice sounded loud in the silence of the night.

"I am. Are you okay, Darbi?" Flynn tried his best to see her face but it was hidden in the darkness.

Darbi shook her head, not quite sure how to respond.

"I'm not sure. I'm cold. Can we keep moving?" She yawned, suddenly tired and hardly able to keep her eyes open. "Is it very far?"

"Not really. About fifteen minutes. I grew up playing in these woods. This is my family's property. I don't get why you were brought here."

Darbi shook her head once more before she laid it against his shoulder.

"I didn't know that. And I don't know why. My aunt and sister and cousins are going to be so worried."

"We'll call them when we get back to my place." Flynn stood, watching as Darbi tried her best to stay awake before he just swept her into his arms. He felt Darbi's arms around his neck before her head snuggled up against his neck and she slept. He froze for a moment, wishing that this was really them, a couple, but knowing that they would walk away from each other. That is, if it was at all possible.

Flynn shoved the door closed with his hip, setting Darbi on her feet and pulling off her jacket. His hand held her upright as his jacket was off and then she was swept back into his arms.

Darbi snuggled down against him, feeling safe and treasured. They had to talk about what had happened, but now was not the time. She just couldn't stay awake.

Flynn stood back after he had laid Darbi on the couch and covered her with a blanket. He left and returned with a pillow from a bed, lifting her head enough to tuck it underneath it. A soft thank you echoed in the room, causing him to smile.

Turning towards the kitchen, Flynn stood at the counter, his hands gripping the edge of it before he reached for the coffee pot, rinsed it out, emptied the old grounds and started a fresh pot. His head turned slightly as he looked towards the doorway. He had no idea what Darbi liked to drink but he hoped that it was coffee. He had no idea how fresh the tea bags here were.

Darbi shot upright two hours later, her eyes huge with fear. She looked around the softly-lit room, taking in the comfort of it. She drew a deep breath of relief. She was safe. She just wasn't quite sure where she was.

Soft footsteps sounded in her ears and she looked towards the sound. Darbi found Flynn walking towards her on socked feet, a tray in his hands.

Flynn grinned at her, knowing that she had questions. He did as well. But first, he had to feed this lady, get a hot drink down her, and then pray with her. That was not an option, praying with her.

—

25

"Darbi? Do you want to clean up some before you eat?" At her nod, he stood, reaching for her hand. "In here. It's my spare room. There are some clean clothes there if you want. My mother was about your size. I just have not had the heart to get rid of anything yet. I haven't been back long enough. She would have wanted you to use them."

Darbi watched him as Flynn stood for a moment, a sober, sad look on his face before he reached to hug her and then closed the door behind him as he left.

The hot water felt wonderful, she decided, as did the clean cloths. She had been through a lot that day and it was not over yet. She stood watching Flynn. He stood at the fireplace, one arm resting on the mantle, the other hand resting on a photo. She really wanted to know who it was but wouldn't ask.

Flynn turned as he heard her footsteps, a welcoming smile covering his face. He walked towards her, his hands out for hers.

"Feel better?" At her nod, he led her to the couch and waited for her to sit. "I have some soup and crackers here. As well as some coffee."

At his hesitation, her hand reached to cover his.

"It's okay, Flynn. We aren't really that hungry, are we?" Darbi stared down at her hands, knowing that they needed to talk. "I need to get home."

"Eat and then I'll drive you there." Flynn didn't want her to leave, not ever. And that surprised him. He had never felt that way before. He didn't believe in love at first sight. At least, he never had in the past.

Chapter 5

Darbi walked towards her home late that night, Flynn keeping step with her. He reached for her keys, unlocking the door and then stepping through as she asked him in. She wandered through her home, surprised to see that someone had been there.

"Someone has been here, Flynn." Darbie almost ran towards him, finding him reaching to hug her. "Who would have done that?"

"Your family? Would they have called the police?"

"I am sure that they did." Darbi shifted in his arms and then looked around. "But it's something different than that. I don't know that I can stay here tonight."

Flynn nodded, knowing that she was correct.

"Go and find some clothes. We'll go back to my place for tonight. It's late. Tomorrow, we'll find your family. It's Saturday. Do you work? And I don't even know what you do." Flynn watched her closely, seeing the moment that she agreed with him even though she didn't say anything out loud.

"I do. I do medical transcription for a company. Today, they were closed or I would already have left before that man appeared. And I still don't know how he got in." Darbi was away, rushing to pack what she needed, reaching for her Bible and then her phone. Shee hesitated as she grabbed it, knowing that she would have multiple messages and texts.

"All set?" Flynn reached for her bag, seeing her hesitation. "It's okay, Darbi. What happened to us? It makes it okay that we're together." He stared down at the ring on her finger and the one on his. Marriage had not been an option that they had been given. The man had made it abundantly clear. Only neither of them knew why. And yes, he thought, they did need to speak about it. Only, that would wait until morning.

The patrol officer watched as Flynn drove away, recognizing Darbi in the car. She's safe, he thought, but I don't know where she is heading. Likely to one of her family. He turned his vehicle, heading for the office to report that he had seen Flynn. Only he had no idea where she was at that point.

Ashlynn turned as she felt a hug the next morning. The three girls had found her as had Gareth and Ronan. Gareth's parents, Garrett and Meg, and Ronan's parents, Ian and Meg, were there as well. The only one missing, she thought, was Frank and Peg. And they were away that day, on a planned holiday for the next week. Frank had apologized but Ashlynn had simply sent him on his way.

She frowned as she heard the door open and then shut. She looked around. The only one missing was Darbi and they had no idea where she was. Ashlynn walked into the entryway, her steps halting as she found her missing niece standing there, a shuttered look on her face before she ran into her aunt's hug. Suppressed sobs shook her body and shook Ashlynn with their intensity.

Darbi stepped back, her hands swiping at her face, feeling Flynn's arm around her for support. She needed that, she decided. They had discussed what had happened. They just didn't know how to explain it to her sister, aunt and cousins.

"Darbi? Where have you been? We have been so worried about you. We looked for you." Ashlynn's attention was then caught by the look on Darbi's face before she looked at the tall man standing so close to Darbi, a protective manner showing clearly.

"Aunt Ash? You did? I'm sorry. I didn't know that. I was taken from my home. Flynn helped me and then we were both taken from his home and walked away. We were kept in an old shack for quite a while until we knew that we were on our own. Flynn led me back to his place. I'm sorry, Aunt Ash." Darbi turned at that moment, burrowing herself into Flynn's arms.

Flynn's eyes were on the lady that he held, before he looked up at Ashlynn.

"I'm sorry that happened to her. I'm Flynn Carson. I am originally from this town but had been living out west for a number of years. I just recently returned." Flynn paused, not quite sure how to proceed with what they had to say.

"Hello, Flynn. Come. We're in the kitchen." Ashlynn paused as she turned, her eyes on Flynn and then her niece as neither made an effort to move. "Darbi?" She realized that Darbi was hiding something. "What is it?"

Darbi looked up at Flynn, seeing his nod, before she looked at her aunt, seeing the others gathering behind her. She sighed. *This is not easy,* she decided.

—

To tell them what we have to and not face the anger and bitterness that will come from it.

"Aunt Ash? I don't know how to tell you this." Darbi bit at her lip, an action that everyone who knew her recognized as uncertainty.

"What Darbi is trying to say?" Flynn simply reached for Darbi's hand, holding it up with his, showing the matching wedding rings. "We were forced to marry yesterday. We don't know why or who made us. We were not given an option."

Silence filled the air at his words, no one sure that what he said was the truth. But the rings on their fingers said that he was, that he and Darbi really were married. Ashlynn looked back at Brinn, seeing the consternation and fear for her sister on her face. She searched the faces of the others, seeing similar emotions.

Ashlynn turned back to the couple before she moved forward, simply sweeping them into her arms and praying for them. Her prayer helped to calm them both. Ashlynn stepped back to let the others move in, her eyes on Brinn. The sisters were close, closer than they may have been in different circumstances. She then looked at Chani and Eilis, seeing their emotions roiling just below the surface.

"Welcome, Flynn, to our family. You're part of it now." Ashlynn stepped back once more, feeling an arm around her.

Ronan had moved closer to her, knowing the emotions that would be roiling in her mind.

"My cousin, Tag and his wife, Ayron, were forced to marry. It didn't matter that Tag was a patrol officer. He was almost beaten to death before he agreed. I'll talk to him, Darbi. I know that he'll reach out to you as will Ayron."

"Thank you, Ronan. That will help. Aunt Ash? Now what?"

"You have spoken with the police?" At Darbi's nod, Ashlyn drew in a wavering breath. "Then, we have some food. We'll spend time in prayer, love, when we're finished."

Chapter 6

Darbi wandered her home late that night. Flynn had simply brought her there, not asking any questions. She could hear him moving around the kitchen and smelt the aroma of freshly-brewed coffee. Flynn would have made her tea as well. Darbi was torn. She knew that they had had no choice in the step that they had taken. They just didn't have any choice in it. That bothered the young couple.

Finding her phone and scrolling through it, Darbi paused at the message from Frank. He and Peg were away, she knew from her aunt, but he had still reached out. Ashlynn must have contacted him, just to let him know that Darbi was home. She shuddered at having to tell him what had transpired.

Flynn stood in the living room, eyeing the room. He liked Darbi's style of decorating and hoped that she would do the same as his house. He sighed. They needed to talk, he knew. Marrying as they had? It would be hard but it was doable, he prayed. Even if Darbi walked away from him and sought an annulment, he would never marry again. He just wished that he had his father there to talk with. Flynn reached for his phone and then smiled. His uncle, Paul, was reaching out to him, just wanting to know if he was okay.

Sending off a quick message, Flynn said no and that he really needed to talk with him. His father wasn't there and he needed some advice. Could they meet tomorrow? His uncle readily agreed, putting aside his phone to stare at his wife.

"Paul? What's wrong?" Sue moved over to sit beside him.

"Something is up with Flynn. He needs to talk and that's not him to ask that."

"No, it's not. All we can do is pray for him right now. I sense that he is going through something hard right now."

"He is. I could hear it in his voice. I was praying that he wouldn't, knowing what some of our young friends from church have faced."

Sue looked at Paul, her mouth opened to speak before she snapped it closed. Paul had been watching her, a good idea of what she was thinking.

"Darbi or Eilis?" His quiet question didn't surprise her.

"Darbi, I would think. What have they gotten mixed up in?" Sue sat back, not ready to sleep, knowing that her nephew needed to be bathed in prayer and that had to happen right then.

Flynn rose early in the morning, a Sunday. He looked around the spare room that he had used, sighing to himself. This was not how he wanted to spend his first Sunday back in his home town. He had planned on skipping church that morning, just because he wasn't ready to face all the questions about his parents. Now, he hadn't a choice. Flynn would be there with Darbi. The questions that they would face would have no answers. At least not yet.

Darbi listened as Flynn moved past her closed door and then descended the stairs. She laid her head back down, her eyes closing as tears flooded them. She raised a hand to wipe them away. She didn't cry, but today she was. Her emotions were all over the place.

Rising and dressing, Darbi hesitated with a hand on the door knob. *Lord, go before us this day. I don't want to face the church family, not when I don't have answers. And especially since I wasn't dating anyone. I know that You are in control and have allowed this. Only neither one of us understands the reasons. You are sovereign. Help my light to shine through this, to be the witness that I need to be. Only I don't see how I can do that.*

Darbi searched for Flynn, not finding him. She shrugged, knowing that he would be around somewhere. Her mug of tea sat waiting for her, doctored just the way that she liked it. Flynn had learned that very quickly. She turned a speculative eye towards the door, hearing voices outside. She walked quickly to the living room window, a smile on her face as she saw Flynn clearing away the snow from the shared driveway, the elderly man who lived next door standing watching him. Mr. O'Rourke would have been out there, struggling to clear his driveway. Darbi knew enough of Flynn's character to know that he would just go ahead and do both.

Ashlynn turned from her own window, a frown on her face. Darbi had not answered her early morning text and that worried her. She sighed. She needed to let go of another one of her girls. Only it was hard to do. It had been easier with Brinn and Chani. They at least had dated their fellows. Darbi didn't get a chance to do that. Ashlynn regretted that. She reached for her phone as it chimed.

"Ashlynn? It's Ayron. Tag got a call from Ronan last night." Ayron was hesitant to question the older lady.

"He did, did he? And he told you what is going on with Darbi?"

"He did. Listen, we're heading that way this morning. We'll talk with Darbi and is it Flynn?"

"It is. I'm not sure where they will be. I'm not sure where they were last night." Ashlynn sighed once more. "It is more difficult this time, Ayron."

"I know it is. I didn't have parents to help me through this. Darbi has you and her sister and cousins. That helps. I was on my own other than for Tag and his friends."

"I know. Come to my place, Ayron. I'll track down Darbi to know where to meet." Ashlynn set aside her phone, reaching instead for her Bible. She needed that, knowing that Darbi had just started off on this walk. Her eyes were on the lamp decoration on her wall. *Lord, help her to be the light for You in all this. I wouldn't have chosen this for her but You did. Help us to help her.*

Darbi turned as she heard the front door open and close quietly and the sound of boots hitting the mat. She drew in a deep breath, knowing that she had to face Flynn, her husband, and she was really reluctant to do just that. They didn't know anything about one another or why they were forced to marry. It just didn't make sense.

Flynn stood, hesitating for a moment before he walked to stand in front of Darbi. His head ducked as he looked into her face, seeing the hesitation on it.

"Darbi? Are you up for church this morning?" Flynn said the first thing that he could and groaned as it did that. That wasn't what he wanted to say. "I'm sorry. I meant to ask if you are okay."

"I am, thank you. And you?" Darbi studied Flynn's face, seeing the stress lines and the fatigue on it. "Did you get any sleep last night?"

Flynn shrugged, not quite sure how to respond.

"Your neighbour is quite the character." He grinned as she snorted.

"Mr. O is at that. He's a widower and looks after me. Thank you for doing his snow. He struggles with it and doesn't like to ask for any help."

"That's what he said. He asked who I was." Flynn bit at his lip. "Do we even know why this happened?"

Darbi shook her head, reaching for his hands. His squeezed hers in response.

"We don't and we need to figure that out. That means calling in reinforcements."

"Reinforcements? As in who?" Flynn was puzzled as Darbi just gave a grin.

"Gareth's parents. Ronan's cousin and his friends. Frank, the investigator who will just take over the case. There are other friends as well who we can reach out to." Darbi paled. "They'll want to know why and what do we tell them?"

"The truth." Flynn turned Darbi towards the kitchen. "Let's find some breakfast and then pray. If you're not up to church this morning, that's okay."

"No, it's not that. It's just all this." Darbi drew in a deep breath. "We need to talk and make decisions. Like where do we live for now."

"We can live here or at my place. It is your choice, Darbi. You make the decision and I will back you. Any decision that you make? I back you, whether I agree totally or not. The only time I don't is if you are in deep danger." Flynn stood tall, strong, and resolute as Darbi looked up at him, shock on her face.

"That's how my parents were. I need my Mom and Dad and they're not here." She began to weep, finding Flynn wrapping her in his arms and weeping with her.

Chapter 7

Flynn walked through his house, not finding anything out of order. That surprised him. He had been certain that something would be out of order. He turned to find Darbi watching him before she walked away, heading for his office. He followed her, not certain what she was up to.

"Darbi?"

"Flynn? I don't get why."

"Neither do I. We need to figure it out. Only it's not what I do."

"I don't know what you do." Darbi spun to face him.

"I'm a journalist, on leave right now. I do have a position here but it doesn't start until the new year. What about you? What do you do?"

"I'm a medical transcriptionist, working out of a building downtown. That doesn't explain why I was kidnapped. You? I could see that."

Flynn grinned even as he heard the doorbell.

"I'll be back, Darbi, and we will finish this conversation." He walked away, a smile on his face as he heard the spluttering from Darbi.

With the door open, Flynn stared at his uncle and aunt before he reached to hug them. Sue held on a little longer, knowing that something was going on with Flynn.

—

"Flynn?" Paul looked at him and then past him as he heard footsteps. A beautiful young lady appeared, hesitating as she saw them.

Flynn turned as he heard Darbi, reaching for her, his arm tight around her.

"Darbi, sweetheart. This is my uncle Paul and his wife, Sue. He's my dad's brother. We need to talk with them."

Sue and Paul shared a look before Sue moved in on Darbi, just enveloping the young lady in a hug before she stepped aside for Paul to do the same.

"Flynn? Is this what you meant when you said you needed your parents?" At Flynn's nod, Paul began to pray for the younger couple, filling Flynn with thankfulness for his family and Darbi with wonder that she had been accepted so readily.

"We need to talk, Flynn." Sue moved towards the kitchen. "Darbi, come with me, dear, if you want. If Flynn will let you go." Sue smirked at her nephew, seeing his grin in return. She knew that it was difficult for Flynn to express his feelings, having been away from them for a number of years.

Paul raised his head at last, his eyes on his nephew.

"Talk to me, Flynn. Tell me what's going on."

Flynn did just that, his hand reaching for Darbi's, finding her fingers curling around his hand. He watched her as he spoke, finding her with her eyes on Paul. She didn't know this couple, a slight frown between her eyebrows.

"That happened? Do you have any idea why?" Paul had reached for a pad of paper and pulled out his pen. He looked down at his notes, not finding a whole lot. "Darbi? You're in healthcare. Did you see something or someone that you shouldn't have?"

Darbi shook her head.

"No, I just work in an office by myself. There are other transcriptionists there but we work independently. In fact, there are a lot of days that I just work from home. As long as the work is done, they really don't care. I normally go in for a least one day a week, just to check in and see if there is anything that I need to know." She shared a look with Flynn. "And I don't have any enemies." She sighed. "That's not true. My oldest cousin and my sister went through something. Each received something from our parents that shouldn't have happened. Brinn received her father's gloves, Chani her mother's music box. We always thought that both sets of parents died in a motor vehicle accident but we found out recently that it was murder. I haven't heard too much on that investigation."

Paul nodded. As a fire captain, he was used to oddities. This, however, involving his nephew was beyond what he had expected.

"Flynn, would someone from the west have followed you?"

Flynn thought about that.

"I'm not sure. They may have. But the men knew the area and used that. Not many people know about that shack on the property."

"No, they don't. Not unless they are familiar with the property. And there are a few of them around. Your father and mother's friends. Your friends. We'll look into that." Paul sat back, his eyes thoughtful.

"We have a friend who will be the investigator." Darbi spoke up at last. "He's away this week. And I have friends who will help. They have all faced danger. My brother-in-law's father is an investigator. I know Brinn talked to him last night. She sent me a text that she had." Darbi grew quiet, a worried look on her face.

Sue nodded. She was a friend of Ashlynn's, knowing her from their Bible study. Although not a close friend, Sue knew Ashlynn well enough that she would be reaching out to her.

"Darbi? What can we do for you at the moment? Right now?" Sue's voice was quiet, filled with love for her nephew's new wife.

Darbi stared at her, not sure how to respond

"I'm really not sure. I just don't know." Darbie pulled her hand back from Flynn's and rubbed at her face. "I just don't know."

Sue rose, an arm around Darbi drawing her to her feet and with her. Sue sat her down on a couch in Flynn's office, her arm still around the younger lady.

"Talk to me, Darbi. For now, think of me as another aunt. I can't and won't replace your aunt, but I do want to help you. We are praying for you both. But for you? What can I pray for?"

Darbi drew in a shuddering breath. She really didn't know what to say. Ashlynn had asked her the same thing the night before. Darbi had had no answer for her either.

"I don't know, Sue. I don't know." Darbi knew that she was repeating herself but was unable to stop it.

"We understand that, Darbi. More than that, God understands. He is here with you. Never stop believing that." Sue prayed for her young friend, knowing that the couple was facing something that no one had that they knew. "We'll need to introduce you two as a couple. That's a given. You can't hide."

Darbi nodded soberly. She and Flynn had talked about that. Neither wanted that but they knew that it was necessary.

"We're meeting with Todd and Nancy tomorrow, just as our pastoral couple. We can make plans, I guess." She blew out a breath. "My family needs to be involved. This hurts."

"It does. How be we meet this afternoon, all of us? We can meet here or at your home or wherever you wish." Sue waited for Darbi to respond.

Darbi stared ahead, not seeing the old oak desk that sat in front of her. This was her home, wasn't it now? She would have to give notice at her own place and pack it up. Only she wasn't ready to do that. Not yet.

"Here, I guess. I'll send out a message to my family. Garrett and Meg will want to be here."

"That's fine. They are your family. Now, your friends who went through this? They will help?"

Darbi nodded, knowing without asking that they would. She sighed to herself. She would need to reach out to others as well. Abe and Emma Finlay were one couple. Another couple would be Doug and Darci Foster. Only she had no desire to do that.

Chapter 8

Flynn turned from the sink late that night. He had finished cleaning the kitchen, something that he did before bed every night. He looked for Darbi, tracking her down in the office, curled up on the couch. He sank beside her, fatigue suddenly hitting hard.

"Darbi? You okay?" Flynn waited, having learned that Darbi would speak when she was ready to and only then.

"I am. Thank you for asking, Flynn. And how about you?" Darbi turned to watch him in the low lighting that she had turned on in the room.

Flynn hesitated before he shook his head.

"No really. I have that headache back. But I am worried about you." He watched her reaction, a frown on his face.

Darbi shrugged, not sure what to say. She had gone over that day in her mind multiple times, unable to determine who the men were or what they wanted. She sighed to herself, her head going down against Flynn without conscious thought on her part.

"What are we to do, Flynn? I'm back to work tomorrow. I have to go in. What are your plans?"

"I'll take you. If it's not a full day, then I'll pick you up."

Darbi nodded, a yawn catching her off guard.

"No, it's not a full day. I only have to be there for only a short time. What will you do?"

"Wait for you." And in his mind, he echoed the words that he would wait for her for the rest of his life. He was falling in love with his bride, without being aware that was happening.

"I see. When does your work start?"

"In January. It's a month to Christmas. Let's pray that this is all over by then. We can enjoy Christmas if it is." Flynn grew quiet as well, his head resting against Darbi as they both slept.

Neither heard the rattling of the doors as they were tried nor the footsteps stomping around the house, marking through the melting snow. All evidence would be gone by morning. Only the feeling that something was wrong would haunt them.

Darbi walked back towards Flynn the next morning. She had been in, done what she needed to, spoken with her employer. He had been surprised at her news but had only given her an intense look. He had watched as she walked away, shaking his head. Darbi was not the one that he ever expected anything to happen to let alone this.

Flynn reached for the bag that she carried, stuffing it into the trunk and then closing the door behind her. He stood for a moment, looking around, feeling someone watching them. He had no idea who it was though.

Darbi was looking too. She saw Ronan watching her and Tag beside him. She waved at them, causing

Flynn to look around. Ronan walked towards them, Tag keeping pace with him.

"Flynn? This is my cousin, Tag. He's the one that we told you about. Can we meet?"

Flynn watched them and then watched Darbi, who nodded. He knew that they were meeting with Todd that evening.

"I guess. Where?" Flynn leaned against his car, his eyes on his keys. He felt shame that he had been unable to prevent the marriage.

Tag had been watching him closely, having a good idea of the gamut of emotions that he would be feeling.

"Flynn? I went through something like this. Only I almost died from the beating. You're feeling a lot of emotions right now. And you are feeling watched. You also have no idea who or why. Is that correct?"

"It is." Flynn was thankful that someone understood. "I want this over for Darbi. It's not fair to her."

"That's how I felt for Ayron. We'll meet later this week. We can work with what little you can tell us. We have a friend who will work this for you. And she never charges friends." Tag motioned to Flynn's car. "Just lead us to where you want to meet."

"Okay." Flynn walked around the car, sliding behind the wheel. He hesitated, not sure what to say or do.

"Flynn? Where are we heading?" Darbi finally broke the silence in the car.

"I'm not sure. Your friends there? They want to meet with us. Which house?"

"How be we head to mine? I need to pack up the perishables in the fridge and take them to yours, if that's where we are going to be living. And I need to pack up my computer and what I need to work." Darbi drew a deep breath, not sure that she was making the right move. "I should tell you that I got a text message. It's nasty."

"Is it? I wondered which one of us would get it. Share it with me and then with the police. They do need to know."

"I know. I just don't like this. Not being on this side of it. I need to talk to both Brinn and Chani, find out what they can tell me. And Ayron. She's a good one for us to talk to. I wonder if she came with Tag."

"She may have. He didn't say. If she had. If not, we'll find her. And we meet with Todd tonight." Flynn didn't know that minister. He was new to the church since Flynn had moved away. "I wonder that I never met you before I left town. Were we not in youth group together?"

"We were. I can remember you, but at that age? I wasn't interested in guys. And I don't think that you were interested in the female species." She smirked at him as he stared at her before his finger was shaking at her.

47

"You have a brutal sense of humour there, sweetheart." Flynn drove towards Darbi's home, not catching the surprised look on her face and then the softening of it as she watched him.

Darbi stood inside her house, not willing to move forward. Something was off. Flynn's hands were on her shoulders. Tag and Ronan shared a look before Ronan reached for his phone, stepping back out of the house to call for help. Tag tapped Flynn's shoulder, his head nodding outside.

"We need to go back outside, sweetheart. We'll need the police to go through. You're feeling something."

"I am." Darbi shoved by him, heading for Ronan, listening to his call. "Someone was in my home. I want to know who and why. We don't need this." Her anger was flaring at the ones who were targeting them.

Tag watched her, a grin on his face. He had expected this, he knew, but Flynn obviously hadn't.

"She has a temper, Flynn. Usually not in evidence. All four of the girls do. Chani's the worst, as you'll find out."

"No, I would not have expected. But I should have." Flynn watched in awe as Darbi paced, her arms wrapped around herself. "You can almost see the sparks, can't you?"

That remark sent Tag off into gales of laughter, bringing Darbi to stand in front of him and glaring at first Tag and then Flynn. Ronan had the sensible decision to stay out of her sight, but his grin was huge.

Chapter 9

Tag rose at last from Darbi's computer, having searched out what he could. He was frustrated at not having enough information to even start a search. He looked for Darbi, finding her in the kitchen, packing up the perishables from the fridge. Ayron stood watching her, her eyes finding Tag. She shook her head. Tag sighed. Darbi was being stubborn, not saying anything.

"Darbi? What do you need done now?"

Darbi froze before she turned, a bleak look on her face. She had not wanted this. She did not want to move from her home. But she obviously had no choice.

"Just to pack up the computer and the printer and what goes with it. Then there's a box of paperwork that I need to take as well." Darbi stood, a hand on her face, her eyes on her aunt as she entered the room. A sob came from her as she threw herself at her aunt, her rock for so many years.

Ashlynn simply hugged her niece hard, her own tears starting. This was not what any of them had expected. She needs her parents, Ashlynn thought, and they are not here.

Darbi stepped back from her aunt, a shamed look on her face, wiping at her face. Ashlynn simply prayed aloud for her, an arm back around her. Ayron picked the prayer as did Tag and then Ronan. Flynn had stepped outside to speak with Mr. O, as Darbi called him, and had missed the torrent of tears.

Flynn walked away at last, heading for his car. He squinted at his watch. They were due at Todd's place in less than an hour and somehow he wasn't sure that they would make it. He turned as he heard footsteps, finding Tag and Ayron walking towards him.

"All set, Flynn? We're off but we'll be back. Send me anything that you need to and we'll look into it. Evan and Shea want to head this way on the weekend, they said." Tag reached to shake Flynn's hand. "Ronan will be around, he said, if you need him."

"Thanks, guys. It's appreciated." Flynn stared at the house, an unreadable look on his face. "I just don't know what to do. We have no idea who it is. There hasn't been much evidence, other than the text message that Darbi got that basically didn't say anything other than ask for some jewels."

"Which she doesn't have." Ayron sighed. "This is where it is hard to trust, Flynn, and trust you must."

Ashlynn paused as she watched Flynn stand at his car, his hand rubbing along the trunk. She had no way of knowing how to help him. She simply hugged him and prayed for him, moving away as he fought for composure.

Darbi turned from her door, knowing that she would not be back there to stay. At least not for a while. That disturbed her to no end. She was growing angry and could now understand what Chani had

---

meant when she described being angry. Her eyes raised to Flynn, finding him watching her, a compassionate look on his face.

"Did you get everything that you needed for now?" He reached for her hand, leading her to his vehicle.

"I think so. I'll need to get my car tomorrow. And I don't feel safe driving any more."

"Ronan asked about it. If you hand him your keys, he'll bring it over for you. He volunteered to do that."

"Okay, I can do that." Darbi stood for a moment. "We have to find Todd and Nancy, don't we? And it's time for you to eat." Darbi was stressed, not sure which way to go. She didn't tell Flynn that she had been getting more text messages and had passed them on to the responding officer from earlier that day. He had promised to let Frank have them when Frank was back.

"Nancy has asked us for a meal. And we will talk about those messages that you don't want to."

Darbi stared at him.

"How did you know?"

Flynn shrugged.

"I just did. I thought that you would be. I'm not. For some reason, they are focusing on you. That's concerning."

"It is." Darbi leaned her arm on the door, cushioning her head on her hand. "I don't like it, Flynn. I want this over and over yesterday."

"So do I. I would like to get to know you better, to take you out for meals and walks and whatnot. Right now, I don't feel safe doing that."

Darbi snorted, bringing a grin to his face.

"We can do that, Flynn. I am not letting them have that much control over me. You can if you want."

Darbi walked towards Todd, who stood outside his house, her hand tight in Flynn's.

"Welcome, Darbi. Nancy is just finishing up our meal. And this is Flynn?"

"It is. You likely know his aunt and uncle." Darbi moved past him, heading for Nancy, leaving Flynn staring after her.

"She's like that, Flynn. Nothing stands in her way if she doesn't want it to. And I do know your aunt and uncle. Your parents as well. I understand that you have work coming up in January?"

"I do. I worked as a reporter out west. I have work here as an investigative reporter waiting for me. Only, I'm not sure any more that's what I want to do."

Todd nodded, understanding what Flynn was saying.

"What you are going through? It can and does change what we want in life. I have not been a victim of any crime, but you and Darbi are. She has lived it with her sister and cousin. We are bathing you both in prayer."

"Thank you, Todd. Any advice that you could give will be greatly appreciated. I'm at a loss right now. We have friends who have offered to help. Only we don't have a lot of information yet. That bothers us both."

"And it will. Experience tells me that it will come in bits and pieces. It will play with your minds, that's a given. And you will worry about Darbi any time that you are not with her. And she will do the same for you. We have friends who will step in if needed. Richard and his team and Don and his team, who are security personnel. Darbi also has a friend from outside of town who has a security team. You will feel smothered if they move in but that would only be if we have a direct and confirmed threat."

"That's what Darbi has said. She said something about a Frank?"

"Frank. He's an investigator with the local force. He worked Brinn and Chani's cases. But he and his wife are also close friends with Ashlynn and knows the girls well."

"I see. That will help. It's just that I am at a loss to explain why we were forced to marry. We didn't know each other. How do we explain it?"

"Tell me what you can. If I have your permission, I'll speak with the church board and deacons. They'll bring it to the congregation, just giving the basics. You will not be judged at all. You will be swamped with offers to help. It's up to you two

—

what help you accept. Now, head on in. Nancy will
be out looking for us for a meal. Once it's done, we
want to pray with you two. That's when you will have
an opportunity to tell us what you can."

Chapter 10

Darbi ran for the back door of the house, her breath coming in gasps. She had simply walked outside five minutes before, needing some fresh air. She had just not expected to find some man approaching her in a menacing manner. She slammed the door behind her, her hands shaking with fear as she shoved the lock on. Dropping to rest against the door, Darbi wrapped her arms around her head. She was so afraid, she decided.

The hammering at the door finally ceased but Darbi was too afraid to stand. She didn't want to see who was out there, to know that he still was waiting for her. She didn't hear Flynn enter and close the front door behind him or hear his calls for her.

Flynn searched for Darbi, not seeing her at first. He heard a sound, a whimpering he thought and frowned. He followed it, finding Darbi still tight to the door. He gave an inaudible sound and was on his knees beside her, pulling her to him.

Darbi fought him until she recognized his voice and wrapped her arms around his neck. She just needed that contact with him, to be made to feel safe.

Flynn shifted on the floor, cradling his bride, his eyes on the door and then her. He sighed as he reached for his phone, struggling to get it out of his pocket. He called for help, not willing to let Darbi go.

Sirens sounded as patrol vehicles raced to their home. A pounding at the front door had Flynn rising reluctantly, setting Darbi on her feet, and heading to let the officers in.

"I don't know what happened. I came home and found Darbi against the back door. She's terrified and hasn't said anything." Flynn was worried, his worry evident to the officers.

Darbi shook her head, not wanting to say anything. Flynn simply held her and nudged her to speak.

"I don't know who he was. He was there in the back yard. I ran for the house and locked the door. He kept trying to get in before he stopped. And no, I don't know who it was. Should I have?" Darbi looked at the officer, looking past him to see Frank walking towards her. "And here's Frank. Has it been a week already?"

"It has been, Darbi. I have all the information that is available. But we need to talk. And talk we will." Frank stopped in front of her before his eyes raised to Flynn. "And you must be Flynn."

"I am. And you are Frank. Welcome home. Now maybe we'll get some answers."

"We'll do our best, Flynn. Darbi, do you know anything?" Frank grinned at her frown.

"No, I don't. If I did, I would tell you. I want this over with and over with yesterday." Darbi walked away, heading back for the kitchen and her tea. "Do what you can, Frank."

Frank simply shook his head, a smile on his face. Flynn stared between the two, not sure what to think.

"It's okay, Flynn. We understand each other, Darbi and I. We'll talk. Let me find the officers and see what they have to say."

Frank walked away, his thoughts troubled for his young friend. That there was no new information available also troubled him. Tag had been in touch, just letting him know that they were working what they could.

Flynn watched Darbi closely, knowing that she was deeply troubled. He sighed to himself. He had had plans to ask her to go out for a meal that night. Now that wouldn't be happening. But he really didn't know what to say or do to help her. Lord? Please?

Darbi paused in making her tea, her hand resting on the kettle. Something was off from today. Had that man really meant her harm or was he trying to help? She thought back on what he had been calling. Her eyes slid closed.

"Flynn? He wasn't after me to harm me. He was trying to help." Darbi turned, finding Flynn's arms open to hug her.

"He was what? You're sure?" He felt her head nodding against him. "Then, we try and find him. How do we do that?"

"I don't know. I guess I can talk to the people down town, the ones on the streets. They usually have a finger on the pulse of the town."

Frank had appeared and paused, hearing their conversation. Her assumption was what he had just discussed with the patrol officers.

—

"Darbi? Are you sure about that?" Frank's voice still her movements before she nodded. "That's what we wondered. We'll look for him."

"How? You don't know what he looks like? I don't have any idea. And we don't have security cameras."

"Which will be rectified tomorrow. Abe said Joseph and Micah are heading this way to do just that." Frank stared her down. "It happens, Darbi. You know that it needs to. Not just for now. Once Flynn starts his new job, word will get out where he lives. People will come around. You two need this for your safety."

"I know, Frank. I know that." Darbi was frustrated. At the moment, she really didn't think that God was listening to her. And she needed to know that. Only, she didn't know how to know for sure. She understood now what Brinn had meant when she said that.

She walked away from the two men, leaving Flynn to walk to the doorway and watch her. Frank headed for the coffee, pouring them each a cup and then turning, his eyes on Flynn.

"Flynn? Talk to me. Did Darbi say anything at all?"

Flynn shook his head before he turned to face Frank.

"Not a word. She's terrified, Frank. And I don't like it. I want this over and over yesterday." Flynn didn't realize that his feelings for Darbi were open on his face.

Frank nodded. It was as he suspected. Flynn had fallen for Darbi and fallen fast and hard.

"She won't say anything, not unless she absolutely has to." Frank looked around Flynn to see Darbi stalking towards him, a box in her hands. "Darbi?"

"Frank. Where did this come from? It was on the desk in the office." She blinked rapidly, almost overcome by her emotions. "It's Mom emerald necklace. The one that came from her parents. How did it appear?"

Frank froze for a moment before he reached for the box. It was as he suspected. There was no note, just the necklace in the box.

"You didn't know that it was missing?" Frank's keen eyes watched Darbi closely.

"I know that we had missed it when we were packing up the house and sorting through things. We thought maybe someone had gotten in and stolen it. I am not sure that we even reported it missing. I would need to ask Aunt Ash."

"And we will. Right now? I'm taking the box. I'll have a tech go over the necklace and then return it to you as soon as I can. You can trust me on that."

"I know that I can. I just don't understand it." Darbi stalked away, her phone out to call her aunt.

Chapter 11

Brinn, Chani, and Eilis walked towards a local cafe, knowing that Darbi was already there. They were not sure how to approach her, not any more. Having her marry like she had? That had changed the dynamics of their group, even though they were together as sisters. That was how they referred to themselves, as sisters, even though they were cousins and sisters.

"Brinn? How is Darbi? I just get text messages from her. She hasn't answered my calls." Chani was worried about her.

"She's okay, sort of." Brinn groaned. "That sounds so definite. She is not really saying. I know that she is scared and worried. She is also angry. I spoke with Flynn this morning. He's worried about Darbi, but can't hover over her. She just won't let him."

"No, she never has done that." Eilis opened the cafe door, looking for her cousin. "She's not here yet."

"She's not? She thought that she would be. Okay. Let's take our usual booth. She'll find us." Brinn turned as she felt a hand on her back, reaching to hug her sister, holding on just a little bit longer.

"You're all here. Where's Aunt Ash?"

"She couldn't make it. She said for us to go ahead with our meal. She'll catch up later." Chani pointed to their booth, heading that way.

Their meal completed, Brinn watched her sister, seeing the tension in her.

"Darbi? Talk to us. What is happening?"

"Right now? Not a lot." Darbi blew out a breath. "I talked to Frank today. That's why I was a little late. He doesn't have enough to go any further with the investigation. Even getting Mom's necklace hasn't helped. He thinks that is related to what you two received."

"It's just bizarre, us getting that kind of stuff. Someone is after all of us." Brinn grew thoughtful before she looked up at a sound from Eilis. "Eilis?"

"Aunt Ash. They're after Aunt Ash and are using us to get to her. Don't you think?" She looked around at the other three.

Chani was nodding.

"Ronan asked that. So have Tag and Ayron. I have to agree that's what's happening."

The ladies enjoyed their meal as best they could but there was much left unspoken and unasked. Darbi sighed. This is not how they were with one another.

Darbi watched as the other three walked away later. She felt lonely and uncertain, not sure where they were heading in this. Flynn had sent a text message just as they were getting ready to leave, just to say that he was thinking about her. What could he do for her? Darbi had just smiled and tucked her phone away. She would see him shortly.

Flynn turned from his garage, searching for Darbi and her vehicle. He thought that she would have been home by now. He sighed to himself. He was just so worried about her and that wasn't the only thing that was on his mind. Preoccupied as he was, he didn't see the man approaching him from behind until he slammed into the garage door. Flynn gave a cry of pain and tried to turn, unable to do so. He felt the slice of the knife as he turned, cutting into his side.

Pain clouded his vision and he dropped to his knees. Flynn didn't hear any sound from the man, only that of his retreating footsteps. He dropped to the ground, blackness crowding in, not letting go of its grip.

Frank's vehicle approached, slowed and then pulled to a stop at the curb. He had no idea why he had come, just felt an urgency to do so. He locked his vehicle as he walked away, searching for what he felt was wrong. A glimpse of a pile of clothes had him hesitating for a moment before he was running towards the garage. His phone was out to call for help even as he did his own assessment of Flynn.

Standing back, Frank eyed the paramedics working over Flynn before he turned away. He walked towards the police line, having been told that Darbi was there. He searched her face before he nodded. There are feelings there, he thought. They're just not ready to say what they are.

"Frank? What's going on? Why can't I go home?" Darbi searched his face, her head beginning to shake.

"Flynn's been hurt, Darbi." His hand was out to steady her. "I don't know how bad yet or what happened. He's unconscious."

"That's not possible. I just got a text from him fifteen minutes ago. Let me go to him." She struggled against the hold that Frank had on her arm. "Frank?"

"You can't, Darbi. It's a crime scene. Here, Joe will take you to the hospital. They're heading off with Flynn."

Darbi took one look at Frank, another at the paramedic rig as it was approached with the stretcher carrying Flynn, and was away and up into it before anyone could stop her. Frank ran after her, sliding to a halt as the paramedics shifted the stretcher in.

"She's riding with us?" The lead paramedic had a puzzled look on his face.

"She is. Darbi and Flynn are married. I'll send a patrol vehicle after you." Frank walked away, shaking his head. Darbi was not acting as she normally did, but he didn't blame her. He likely would have done the same if he had been in her shoes.

Ashlynn reached for Darbi, just wrapping her into her arms. She felt the sobs shaking Darbi's body, knowing that she was also scared for Flynn. They had had no word yet on his condition and that was something Ashlynn wanted to rectify. Only, she had to stay back. *Lord, heal this young man. He means the world to my Darbi. I can see that. And she has his heart. Only, they're afraid to say anything, aren't they? I don't know why they are going through this, but You do. It is for Your glory. Bring them through*

—

Darbi paced, unable to sit. She didn't see Gareth
and Ronan pacing with her or that Paul and Sue had
appeared. She was just too focused on Flynn and what
was wrong with him. Frank had been around,
observing her before he walked away, this time for the
examination room area.

Gareth's hand on her arm stopped Darbi and she
jumped, not knowing that he was there.

"Darbi? Frank is out here again. He wants to
speak with you." Gareth nodded towards where Frank
was standing just a few feet from her.

"Frank? What can you tell me? Is he alive?"
Darbi wrung her hands together, not a move that
anyone who knew her recognized. This was the stress
that she was under coming out.

"He is, Darbi. He's awake. Right now, the
surgeon is assessing him. Come, I'll take you back.
Who do you want with you?"

"With me? I'm not sure that I understand?"
Darbi looked around at her family, finding Brinn and
Ashlynn moving in on her. "Brinn? Aunt Ash? What
does he mean?"

"He means that we need to be with you. Just for
support." Ashlynn's arm was around her niece,
following as Frank led the way back.

Darbi hesitated at the door before she was almost
running across the room, reaching for the hand that
Flynn held out. She didn't care that it was shaking

---

from pain or that his face was white and drawn. All she cared about was that he was alive and still here with her. Sobs shook her body even as she gripped his hand as tight as she could.

Chapter 12

Flynn moved restlessly late that night. He had not been allowed home, much to his dismay. He wanted that but Darbi had over ruled him and insisted that he stay. He watched Darbi as she was curled up in a chair, a blanket wrapped around her. He sighed. Flynn wanted out of there and to protect his lady. He needed to find out who had assaulted him and then bring them to justice.

Darbi watched him through her lowered eyelashes. She was afraid for him, not sure where they were heading as a couple, but not wanting him to be hurt again. Not if it related to her.

Frank hesitated as he stood outside the room. He needed to speak with Flynn but he had wanted to do that without Darbi present. That would not happen, he knew. Darbi would be right in there in the midst of everything.

Flynn looked up as he heard a sound, fear on his face. He breathed a sigh of relief as he saw that it was Frank.

"Frank? You're here. It's late." Flynn squinted at his watch. "It's almost 11."

"I know. I'm on call overnight. So how be you talk to me and tell me what happened?" Frank leaned against the end of the bed. He had no idea what Flynn went through but he needed to know.

"I don't know, Frank. I was outside the garage, waiting for Darbi. Then I was shoved against the door, a knife slashed me, and I collapsed. Do you know who it was?"

"No, we don't. There was nothing there to say who or why. When are your security cameras going in?" Frank narrowed his eyes as he caught a movement from Darbi. "Darbi?"

"They are going in on Monday. We didn't think anything would happen." Darbi shoved away the blanket and walked away, leaving the two men staring after her.

"She shouldn't have done that." Frank was after her and brought her back. "Don't run on me, Darbi. They can nab you at that point and you could disappear on us."

"I know. Maybe that's what I want. To disappear and find them." Darbi was becoming belligerent.

Flynn stared at her, not sure that he had heard her correctly. His gaze shifted to Frank, finding Frank with a grin on his face.

"That's not what you want, Darbi. You know that. You can do this, you know."

"I know. This time? It's different. We need this over with. Flynn needs to go on with his life. And which one of us are they after? Do you know that?"

"No, we don't, Darbi. I wish I could tell you that we did and that we had arrested them. That has not happened as yet." Frank stayed for a while longer, assessing the couple. He walked away at last, heading

—

for another crime scene, knowing that he felt he had failed them.

Flynn raised himself to the side of the bed, holding on to his side. The knife had cut deep but not deep enough to do damage. He would heal physically. Mentally? That was another question that he wouldn't answer right then.

"Flynn? What are you doing?" Darbi stared at him before he simply swept her into his arms. Darbi struggled for a moment before she rested against him.

"I'm heading home, Darbi. Head out to the nurse and get my discharge papers. I'll meet you out there." Flynn dropped a kiss on her temple and then watched as she walked away, hesitating in the doorway to stare back at him.

Flynn sighed as he walked through his house. Maybe this wasn't such a good idea, he thought. Darbi stood and watched him, walking away at last to head for bed. Obviously, Flynn was okay, she thought

Flynn dropped down into his desk chair, pain on his face. He had tried to hide it but was unsuccessful. He prayed that Darbi was safe and asleep before his head went down on his folded arms. He wept, just needing his parents but not having them there. He slept at last, not hearing Darbi moving around early the next morning. Darbi stood beside him, her hand resting on his head, praying for him. She did not pray for herself. That was not something that she was accustomed to doing.

Moving away from him, she reached for a blanket, wrapping it around him an dropping a kiss on

—

his cheek. She left, standing in the hallway for a moment, watching him, seeing in him the knight that her mother had woven into her bedtime stories. Only, she didn't think that he would stay. Not with the way that they had married.

Hearing a tap at the door, Darbi's hand went to her throat as she crept forward, to peek out of the door. She frowned for a moment before she opened it.

"Joseph? Luke? What are you two doing here today? You weren't to be here until tomorrow." She hugged them and then stepped back, seeing their ladies walking up behind them.

"Abigail? Leah? I didn't expect to see you two. Your children?"

"They're with our families. Today, we are here for you." Joseph nodded towards the kitchen. "Abe talked to Frank last night. He sent us today, knowing that you needed this security stuff installed."

"Security stuff? Is that what it's called?" Darbi grinned at them. "Go ahead. Just watch the office. Flynn is sleeping at his desk. He never made it to bed last night, not that I can see."

Joseph shared a look with Luke and then nodded.

"We'll get busy then and leave you three ladies to talk. Is your family heading this way at all?"

"I have no idea." Darbi's hands flew into the air. "I haven't checked my phone yet today. I've been avoiding it." She looked sheepish at that.

"Let me see it, please, Darbi." Luke held out his hand. "You've been receiving messages and photos?"

—

At her nod, he nodded himself. "We went through that, Darbi. You have heard our stories. You know that is how it works given what Brinn and Chani went through. To say nothing of Tag and his friends."

"I know. I just don't have to like it." She almost slapped her phone into his hand and then looked contrite. "I'm sorry. This has not been a good day as yet."

"No, it won't have been. With all that's going on, you're confused, scared, terrified, worried. And you find yourself in a situation not of your making and without a choice. You really didn't have a choice to marry Flynn, now did you?" Abigail's arm was around Darbi as she turned her to the kitchen.

"No, we didn't. They just showed up with a minister, who looked as if he was scared too, and made us marry. I just don't understand. They had a license. That meant that at some point they had our identification." Darbi stopped in her tracks at that thought.

"It does. And unfortunately, that can happen. This was planned, Darbi. Not a spur of the moment thing. That means that they have been watching you both, following you." Leah looked around at her, reaching for the coffee pot.

"It does. And who does that?" Darbi wrapped her arms around herself in a defensive manner. "I had never met Flynn. I mean we did go to the same youth group as teens but we never spoke to one another. Not that I remember. How long has this been planned?" She turned to stare at the open doorway. "And what he went through out west? Could someone have done that to make him move back here?"

Abigail and Leah shared a look.

"That's what Emma has asked. She's starting to work her magic. And she said Evan had asked if he could as well. Between then, they'll find the answers."

"I am sure that they will." Darbi's eyes were on Flynn as he stood in the hallway, not entering, just listening to their conversation. "And here is Flynn. Do you want coffee first, Flynn, or to clean up?"

Flynn nodded at her.

"To clean up, I think. Then, we talk. I want to know who Emma is and why she would ask that."

Chapter 13

Flynn stood in the kitchen, mug of coffee in hand, listening to the ladies talk. He shoved away from the counter and wandered through his house, finding Joseph in his office. He had no idea where Luke had disappeared to.

"Flynn? What can you tell us about what's going on?" Joseph turned for a moment from where he was running wires at the window.

"Not a lot. I don't know why we were taken or forced to marry. It doesn't make sense. I am not aware that I had any enemies here in town. And I don't think that Darbi does."

"There has to be something connecting you two. Have you two known each other all your lives?"

"No. We haven't. I mean we went to the same youth group, but I was older than her. We went to different schools. I moved west to go to school and then worked there. She's been here in our town." Flynn slumped at his desk, a hand holding up his head. The other arm was wrapped around his abdomen, trying to control the pain.

"There has to be something. Emma is working on it, she said, but hadn't found anything. How about your parents?"

"I lost both of them to cancer within a few months of one another. So I don't know if there was anything there. Emma can speak with my uncle Paul, if she likes. He might have an idea."

Luke walked towards them, a grim look on his face. He had been outside, just walking the property to see what they could do to make it safer. A letter was in his hand.

"Flynn, I just found this on your garage door. It wasn't there when we arrived."

Flynn nodded as he reached for it.

"Frank warned me about these. Darbi said that she had been getting text messages."

"She has been. I've seen them. Nothing to say who it was. We'll look into them. Micah was starting that." Luke sat for a moment, praying for Flynn and Darbi.

Flynn stared down at the letter before he opened it. He stared at the photos that fell out.

"This is strange. Photos from the hospital. They were there, weren't they?"

"They were. It's a public place and we can't keep them out. That's not possible." Luke reached for them, studying them and then handing them back. "Nothing in there that is threatening, is there?"

"No, just random photos." Flynn looked up as he felt Darbi's hand on his. "Darbi?"

"They're starting this? I thought at some point they would. How do we stay safe?"

"It's not easy, Darbi." Luke shared a look with Joseph. "Even though we are trained in keeping people safe, we still went through some pretty hard stuff. All

---

of us on our team. You have met Doug and Darci and know their story.”

“I do. It was brutal. Darci said a number of your other friends went through danger.” Darbi perched on the arm of Flynn’s chair, her arm around his neck. She felt his arm around her. “Tell us, Luke. Joseph. Tell us how we do this. I know what Brinn and Chani went through but theirs were different from each other.”

“They were. So, what can we tell you?” Joseph tucked away his tools, done with running his security system. He just needed to test it. “Stay alert. Be with someone if you can when you are out and about. Flynn, you said that your work didn’t start until the new year?”

“That’s correct. I have spoken with the publisher. He’s willing to work with me. I didn’t know at the time but he was a schoolmate of my father’s. He doesn’t want to see me hurt.” Flynn paused, not sure how to continue.

“And you, Darbi? You’re still working?” Luke took up the question, his eyes on Abigail as she and Leah tracked everyone down.

“I am. I only go into the office once a week but I really don’t need to do that. My boss is fine if I don’t. I can email what I need to.” Darbi’s face grew dark. “I just don’t want to give that up.”

“You may need to for now. Just until we get this sorted out. Emma said that she was reaching out to Frank.”

—

"She will, I know." Darbi slumped against Flynn, missing his wince.

The other four shared a look with one another, knowing that Flynn was hurting and needed to rest. Only they knew that he wouldn't.

"What does Emma do, Joseph? I keep hearing her name but I have never met the lady." Flynn looked around at the soft laughter. "Did I say something funny?"

"No, you didn't, Flynn. Emma has a business where she tracks down people. She finds people no one else can find. She can't explain how she does it. And Darci will come up with a profile for you. She's a retired forensics psychologist." Luke shook his head, a grin on his face. "She can do that without meeting you two or even having a suspect. She'll pass that on to you two and to Frank as well. And she will be bang on with her description."

"I see." Flynn studied them and then Darbi, finding her face thoughtful but he could tell that she was not in the room with them. "So, what do we do then? I can't be with Darbi all the time."

"We realize that." Abigail fished into a pocket, pulling out a cloth bag. "Micah has worked his magic again. When Luke and I were going through our adventure, he came up with a bracelet that let them trace me. It worked. So, he has come up with a bracelet for Darbi. It is tied into his program but he will forward it to you both so that you can download it to your computers and your phones. For you, Flynn, he came up with a ring. You don't normally wear one but this one is necessary." She showed them how to activate them and then turn them off.

Joseph was staring at their wedding bands.

"Who provided the rings?"

Flynn stared at him, his face turning white.

"They did. Do you think that there is some sort of tracking device in them?"

"It is possible. We've seen it before. I would suggest that you invest in new rings tomorrow and then hand those off to Frank or his team. They can tell you if something is there." Joseph looked around, satisfied with what he had done.

"Okay, so we do that." Flynn sighed, growing tired of being up. "What else?"

"For now, we set you up with a really good password. I have the program on your computer. We have also tied it into ours for now so that if someone does get through, we'll get a notification and send help."

"That works." Darbi was on her feet, heading for the door, hearing a knock. She pulled it open to find her aunt and sister and cousins there. "What are you doing here?"

"We have come to see you." Ashlynn grinned, reaching to hug her. "But you have company."

"Just some of Abe's men and their wives. They have set up a security system for us." Darbi looked distraught for a moment. "Aunt Ash? Who would do this? Who did I see that I shouldn't have or what did I see that I didn't know was wrong?"

"That we will work on. For now, we want to pray with you two. And share a meal. Will Abe's fellows stay?"

"We would like to, Ashlynn." Luke spoke from behind Darbi. "But we need to get on the road. We've a full load of trainees in tomorrow and have to meet tonight."

Chapter 14

A week had passed, bringing no response to any inquiries that Frank had put out. The streets were silent, which was unusual. Usually he could find some sort of information. That told him that the people were afraid. Just what they were afraid of he wasn't sure.

Darbi tracked him down one day at Jeff's diner, sliding into the seat across from him. She accepted with thanks the mug of tea set before her. Frank watched her, seeing the subtle signs of fear and stress in her.

"How are you, Darbi?" Frank spoke at last, his eyes on his plate.

"Not well. I want this over. Flynn needs his life back." Darbi blew out a breath. "We haven't been getting any more text messages or photos. No packages. Isn't that what they usually do?"

"It is but they are likely keeping a close eye on you. Any activity on the security system?"

"No. Joseph has been in touch. They've been monitoring for us and said the same thing. That has them puzzled." Darbi stared down at the engraved rose gold ring that Flynn had chosen, matching it with an emerald engagement ring. She had protested at that but he had simply shaken his head, continuing to slide it on her finger.

"They will pick up their activity. I find sometimes they do this, go silent. It's harder on you when they are silent. That plays on your minds."

Frank sat back, starting past Darbi, a frown on his face. "I can't figure it out, Darbi, to tell you the truth. Flynn doesn't have any enemies that we know of."

"We know that, Frank. He's going back over all the stories that he did out west. He thinks maybe someone from there has followed him. Flynn did say that he felt followed out there but that was normal for them, he said. There was always someone doing that."

Frank nodded, having had the same thought.

"Have him call me with any names that he feels might be someone who he suspects." Frank leaned forward, his arms on the table.

"He's trying to make a list but it's tough. He really doesn't remember a lot about anyone who threatened him. He's reaching out to his previous employer." Darbi shrugged into her jacket, dropping money on the table for her tea.

"Let me walk you out, Darbi." Frank stood and followed her out, a hand to her back as he directed her towards her car.

The sudden squealing of tires had Frank spinning and then shoving Darbi towards his car. They ran for it, hoping and praying to make it. Frank slid to a stop, an arm around Darbi to keep her on her feet as the car squealed to a halt in front of them. His hands raised as he saw the gun pointed at him.

Darbi's head was moving as she looked for a way out. Only, she couldn't see one. *Lord, this would be a good time for a rescue. I can't see any way out for us.*

Frank shoved Darbi behind him, watching the man in front of him. Something told him that they would not make it out, at least without injury. His hands went back up as he searched the area. He could hear commotion behind him and heard the sounds of voices. He wouldn't turn, his attention focused on what was in front of him.

The man facing Frank didn't say anything. He simply raised his gun and pulled the trigger. Frank flew backwards, Darbi falling with him. A cry was torn from her even as she found her hands and knees and scrambled away, hoping and praying to get away. She felt the burn of the bullet that struck her and collapsed. Neither one heard the slamming of the car door and the sound of the motor as it revved before the car raced away. They didn't hear the cries of the men and women who ran to their aid.

Ronan had been headed there with Tag, out for a meal with him, when he saw the car racing away.

"I don't like this, Tag."

"Nor do I." Tag looked around, pulling Ronan to one side. "Were any of the ladies here today?"

"Not that I know of." Ronan moved to where he could see the scene in the parking lot. He searched the vehicles ad paled. "Darbi!"

"Darbi? She's here?" Tag stared at his cousin and then back at the scene. His heart dropped. As a former officer, he had responded to too many scenes likes this.

"She is. Her car's here. Please, Lord, let her be safe!" Ronan moved as close as he could, shouldering through the onlookers to stand and stare at the scene, not knowing if Darbi was hurt or if she had just left her car there while she shopped elsewhere.

Frank was rolled to his back, frantic hands shoving towels on the wound. Blood from it covered the right side of his chest. His breathing was erratic and onlookers feared for his life. They moved aside as paramedics moved in.

Darbi lay still, her eyes open, shock evident on her face. She had not expected to be shot. Not at all. She didn't respond to the questions asked her and ignored the feel of hands on her leg, cutting away her jeans and pushing packing and bandages on the wound to control the bleeding.

Lifted to a stretcher, Frank was wheeled almost on a run to a waiting paramedic rig. The jolting as it was lifted caused him to groan but he did not rouse.

Ronan's heart sank as he watched the lady lifted to the stretcher. He recognized Darbi's jacket. His hand reached out for Tag.

"It's Darbi. She's hurt." Ronan spun, intent on finding Brinn and then Ashlynn.

"Ronan, wait. We don't know what happened yet."

"No, we don't but I need to find Brinn and Ashlynn and Flynn." He hesitated, not sure who to run to first.

"Ronan, in." Tag shoved him into his truck and ran for the driver's side. "We'll find Flynn and then Brinn and Ashlynn. Wait. Call Brinn. Just tell her that she needs to go to the hospital. You think that Darbi is hurt but you're not sure, that you're on your way there."

Flynn stood in shock as Ronan shoved his jacket at him. *It wasn't possible,* he thought. *She was only going down town for a while. Lord? Is she hurt? Is my lady in danger? Please, Lord, I can't handle losing her. Please, Lord.*

Chapter 15

Flynn perched on the edge of a chair, his focus only on the doors behind where his bride lay. Neither Tag nor Ronan could tell him what had happened. The only thing that the clerk could tell him either was to confirm that Darbi was there and being seen. He didn't feel the arm that came around his shoulders.

Ashlynn had stared at Ronan as he had approached her, simply reaching for her purse and coat, almost running to his car. Chani had been there, tears on her face.

"Brinn? Eilis?" Ashlynn could ask nothing more.

"Tag was reaching out to Gareth and then Eilis. He'll make sure that they get there." Ronan had sped through the streets, finding them strangely empty for that time of the morning. "Someone else was hurt but I don't know who."

Ashlynn studied the waiting room, wondering that some many officers were milling around.

"Aunt Ash? What's going on? Was an officer hurt?" Brinn shared her aunt's thoughts.

"I wonder, Brinn." She looked up as she heard footsteps and saw Peg being rushed into the exam room area. "Oh, no! There's Peg!"

"Frank?" Chani turned to Ronan, finding his arms and comfort from them. "Ronan? Did you know?"

"No, we didn't, sweetheart. We just knew that there were two injured." Ronan nodded as Tag caught his eye and then moved away to speak with an officer who he knew. He saw the tightness on his cousin's face. Frank was injured and badly by the looks of it, he thought.

Brinn was watching Peg as she disappeared and drew a deep breath.

"It's Frank, isn't it?"

Ashlynn nodded, knowing that it likely was. She prayed for her friend, not sure what would happen. She wrapped her arm around Brinn an pulled her closer, seeing Gareth standing with Ronan and Tag, his eyes on his wife before he raised them to Ashlynn and then over to Flynn.

Flynn rose and began to pace, mingling among the officers who were there. Most knew who he was, having heard of him from Frank. They looked out for him, knowing that was what Frank would have asked of them.

Ronan finally stepped into Flynn's path, stopping him with his hand on Flynn's arm. Flynn stared at him before his eyes closed. His emotions were just too raw. Ronan drew him aside to a sheltered corner, Tag and Gareth stepping in to provide shelter from prying eyes. Paul walked towards them, his arm coming around his nephew, feeling the sobs shuddering in the younger man's body.

"Flynn? Can you tell me what happened?" Paul didn't pry, didn't push, just waited for Flynn to speak. That was something he had in common with Flynn's father, Peter. Both men would ask and then wait for Flynn to talk. That always happened. Flynn had always appreciated their not pushing him to talk.

"I don't know, Uncle Paul. Ronan came and found me. He told me that he thought Darbi was hurt. I spoke with the clerk but they haven't let me back in there yet." Flynn moved into his uncle's hug, hearing his low-spoken prayer. He then felt his aunt's arms around him and began to weep, his sobs shaking him at their intensity before he stepped back, wiping at his eyes.

Ronan turned as he heard footsteps and moved aside so that the nurse could move in to speak with him.

"Flynn? Come with me. The doctor wishes to speak with you." The nurse waited, compassion on her face, watching as Ashlynn and Brinn moved in. "Ashlynn? If it's okay with Flynn, you two can come as well."

Flynn moved towards the stretcher, his hand out to rest against Darbi's white face. She stirred, her eyes opening as she glanced around. He could see the fear on her face.

"Darbi? Sweetheart? We're here." He bent over the bed and kissed her forehead and then stepped back as Ashlynn and Brinn moved in.

He felt the anger growing in him at whoever it was who had done this. He turned as he felt someone beside him.

The surgeon stood there. He had known Flynn's parents years previously. Flynn had been a friend to his son. They had not reconnected yet since Flynn had moved back home.

"Flynn? Let me speak with you." David Walker laid a hand on Flynn's shoulder. "Darbi is a fortunate young lady. God had His hand on her."

"How bad, David?" Flynn refused to look away from Darbi.

"She was hit in the leg. We think that she was moving away from the shooter when she was hit. That being said, she will need surgery. We can't see that there is a lot of damage to any major blood vessels or the bone."

"How long a recovery, David?" Flynn sighed. "I'll have to set her up on the main floor. She won't be climbing stairs for a while."

"No, she won't. Recovery depends on how she heals. I know that doesn't help. Only God knows how long a recovery she will have. You are in our prayers, son."

"Thank you, David. I have felt those prayers over the years. The thing is, we are the targets of someone. Only we have no idea who. We'll need to watch her carefully." Flynn bit at his lip, not sure how to proceed.

"That has been taken care of. Richard was here for another reason, visiting someone, and heard. He has brought in his team."

—

"Frank? Is he okay?" Ashlynn had approached, waiting as Flynn signed the consents.

David hesitated, not knowing how to answer.

"It's okay, David. We know that you can't say. We're praying for him and Peg." Ashlynn drew Brinn away, leaving Flynn to walk back to his wife.

Flynn had no intention of leaving until he had to. He reached for Darbi's hand and then leaned on the bedrail, his eyes not moving from her face as she slept, pain evident on her beloved face.

Richard stood in the doorway, sorrow flowing through him. He had not expected to have to move in and provide protection for another one of the Whitman ladies. Silver had stepped into the room and stood near the bed. The other three team members were around somewhere close. His head turned as he heard hurried footsteps and watched as Frank was rushed towards the elevators, heading for surgery. His prayer went with him and then went up for Peg.

Chapter 16

Peg stood at the ICU doorway, worried about Frank. He had been through surgery and they were settling him now. She knew his condition was grave. She hadn't needed to be told that. Ashlynn had found her at one point, sitting with her, just being silent and praying for her.

Able at last to walk into Frank's room, Peg drew a deep breath. They both knew the dangers of Frank's job and had accepted those risks, the risks that had never come true until now. She watched as he slept under the grip of the anesthesia, the beep and hum of the machines sounding in her ears.

Leaving when asked, Peg had walked away, looking for someone, anyone who could just be with her. They had no children and their families were gone. She turned as she felt an arm around her. Eilis had found her and drew her with her.

"Come, Peg. You need to eat something, even just have something to drink. We have that waiting for you."

Peg nodded, her eyes on Eilis, seeing the strain on her face.

"Eilis? Darbi? How is she?"

"Darbi? She's awake or was. She wants to come home."

"And she will. How bad was she hurt?"

"Nowhere near as bad as Frank was. She had to have surgery to repair the muscle that was torn and the blood vessels that were damaged. She'll be here for a couple of days."

"I see. And Flynn? How is he?" Peg watched Flynn as he sat, his head buried in his hands.

"He's hurting, Peg. I can't say anything more than that. We need to find out who did this. Not just for Darbi but for Frank."

"And we will. We have people working on it who will do just that. Now, what can we do for you, Peg?" Ashlynn reached to hug her friend of many years.

"You are doing that, Ashlynn. We have felt your prayers over the last hours."

The group was quiet, lost in their own thoughts or deep in prayer. Richard's team moved among them, Silver and Naomi staying with the group. Stephen and Timothy moved through the hospital and the outside of it, keeping in touch with Richard as he spoke with the authorities about what had happened. He had been shocked to hear that the attempt on his friends' lives had been made so openly. That concerned them all.

Darbi roused in the early morning hours, staring around. She gave a small moan as she moved, her hand finding her thigh and the thick bandages there. She turned her head, staring at the equipment surrounding her, raising her hand to stare at the IV line running to her hand. Darbi jumped as she felt someone touch her face before she leaned into the touch. *Flynn,* she thought. *He's found me. And is he safe and well? I don't remember what happened. I need to but I'm afraid to.*

Flynn watched his beloved Darbi closely. He had thought that he had lost her and just couldn't bear that thought. It was too soon to tell her how he felt but at some point he would.

"Darbi?" Flynn's voice was quiet. He had just refused to leave, staring down the nurse who suggested that he needed to.

"Flynn? What happened? I hurt. All over." Darbi's eyes slid closed and she slept. Her hand tightened on Flynn's, not letting him escape.

"You scared me is what happened, dearest Darbi. I thought that you were gone. And I can't lose you. Not yet. We've just begun our journey." Flynn hooked his foot around his chair and pulled it closer, sitting where he could watch her face.

Naomi peeked in before she approached Flynn, her eyes flickering between the couple.

"Flynn?"

Flynn shook off her sadness, looking up at Naomi.

"She was awake, Naomi. Just long enough to ask what happened and state that she hurt." Flynn studied his bride once more. "I'm taking her home today. David said it was all right. Her family is going to be in and out, helping her. I just want whoever it was just as I know that Peg does. When does this end, Naomi? When one or both of us are dead? Is that what they want? I don't have anything that anyone would want.

I brought nothing back from the west. I didn't do crime reporting. So, how do we find out what they want?"

"Emma is working on that but she's not finding out a lot. And that is very unusual for her. She always finds the people responsible for whatever it is."

"I know. She called me last night, just to talk. I want to meet her and her husband."

"And you will. I know Luke and Joseph were around. The other five will be here at some point. And I know that Ian will want to fly you somewhere no one can find you."

"He'd do that?" Darbi had to clear her voice to be heard. "I want that. Tell him to come today and do that." She was asleep again before either one with her could speak.

Naomi began to laugh at the expression on Flynn's face.

"Did she really just do that?" Flynn was astounded to say the least.

"She did. And he would. If he thought it would help, Abe would send him. I know that Abe and Richard have been talking. For now, Flynn, we are your shadows. Not close but we will be around you. And if we can't, then a friend, Don, will move in with his team."

"We can't do that!" Flynn stared at her, shock on his face. "We can't afford that. Tell them to stay away!"

"They won't, Flynn. Darbi's a friend of theirs and that makes you a friend as well. And they never bill friends. That's how it is. They have said that God has blessed in to many ways that it is doing His bidding to help friends."

Flynn mulled that over before a small frown crossed his face.

"That's a good way of looking after. I have done some research on a foundation near here. They work as encouragers to others, just as Barnabas was to Paul. I think I need to go see them and talk to them. It would make an interesting story."

"It is an interesting story, but I don't know that they would talk with you. I mean, it's out there what they do and how they help. I would contact Barnabas or Breck there."

"You know them." It wasn't a question but a statement that Flynn made.

"We do. They are a blessing to many."

Chapter 17

Darbi was grateful to be home but frustrated that she had been shot. She had asked about Frank, sorrow on her face as she had heard how seriously that he had been hurt. She knew that Flynn was hovering over her and would allow him that for the day. But then she decided it needed to end after that.

Flynn hesitated to approach Darbi. His feelings had intensified for her over the previous hours. He was afraid that he would chase her away if she found out how much he cared.

"Darbi? What can I get for you?" Flynn was beside her, a hand on hers, just waiting and watching.

"I don't know, Flynn. I really don't." Her head went back on the couch as her eyes closed. A single tear tracked down her cheek and he reached to wipe it away. "I hate that Frank was hurt."

"And he would have done nothing different. He would have done his best to protect you." Flynn reached to wrap her in his arms, nodding at Brinn as she dropped a tray on the table in front of them and then sat. "Did they ask for anything?"

"Not that I remember. I don't remember them saying anything. Or him. There was only one who got out of the vehicle. Frank was moving me backwards when he was shot. He never had time to reach for his own weapon."

"And he would have, had he had a chance. He was trying to get you away and to safety. It's ingrained in him as a person and as a police officer." Brinn sat back, her eyes on her sister. "Darbi? Have you thought any more about Mom and Dad?"

"Not really. I mean, I have but not about what happened to them. I think I'm in denial right now. We thought for so many years, over half of our lives, that they were killed in an accident. Then, we find out that they weren't, that they were murdered. And we have no idea by whom or why."

Brinn nodded, feeling the same. Flynn was watching Darbi, seeing the fatigue on her face, but knowing that she just wouldn't go to bed. He dropped a kiss on her temple and then rose, to walk away. He had some work that he needed to be at, that should have been done yesterday, but hadn't been. Darbi came first and always would.

"How is Frank?" Dari was almost afraid to ask.

"He's alive, Darbi, and stirring somewhat, Peg said. This means a new investigator for you."

"And I don't like that." Darbi winced as she moved, the pain in her leg stopping her for a moment. "It was just so strange. The car pulled up. The man got out and then just stood there. He shot as Frank moved me away. I think that was the purpose all along. Take out Frank and then bring in someone new. How do we trust someone new?"

Brinn nodded. She and Gareth had discussed that between themselves. Garrett had weighed in as well, simply stating that it was odd.

"I think that's what it was. Only because a cop was shot, they'll be more of a target to find. This is not being taken lightly." Brinn's eyes slid closed for a moment as she prayed. She heard footsteps heading their way and looked around the back of the chair.

Ashlyn, Chani, and Eilis stood there for a moment before they all found seats. Ashlynn simply bowed her head and began to pray. The younger ladies followed her example. Brinn looked around again as more footsteps sounded, and Gareth, Ronan, and Flynn appeared, trays with food and fresh tea and coffee on them.

Darbi was not hungry, instead feeling grubby and sore. She stared at the mug of soup, sipping at it absentmindedly. She listened to the conversation, a puzzled look on her face. Garrett and Meg had shown up as had Paul and Sue.

Garrett studied her before he spoke.

"Something is puzzling you, Darbi. Talk to us."

Darbi nodded thoughtfully.

"I'm not sure how to express what I want to say." She sighed, her eyes on Garrett. "If I just say what I need to or think, does that work?"

"It does, Darbi. We'll make sense of it. Before you go ahead, Abe has been in touch. He and Emma will head this way over the next couple of days. Apparently, Doug and Darci will come with them. They feel it is necessary."

"They are? Of course, they are." Darbi snuggled down against Flynn, finding him holding her close to him. She sought comfort from him, finding that and also feeling that he cared for her and treasured her in how he held her.

"They are. Now, just say what you need to, Darbi. We'll make notes and then go from there. You need to do this and then get some sleep." Garrett shared a look with Flynn, who nodded.

Flynn had been able to set up a room for Darbi on the main floor. He was thankful that his parents had installed a three-piece bathroom just off the office. That would work, he thought, and be easier for Darbi to manage.

"Okay. So, yesterday. The man never asked for anything. He simply stepped out of his car and held a weapon on us. I don't really remember there being much conversation. Frank was walking me back to my car. I think he expected something to happen.

"He shoved me behind me and then tried to run with me. That's when he was shot. When he fell, I fell. I tried to get to my feet and didn't have time. The vehicle? A high-end, expensive one. Black with heavily tinted windows. The man was medium height, stocky. He wore a navy blue suit with a white shirt and pink tie. That was so odd, the colour of the tie. And he had a goatee. Balding somewhat. Gray hair. I didn't see his eyes but I think they were light colour. They were cold. That much I know."

"That's good, Darbi. Now, were you able to see how many were in the car?"

Darbi's brow furrowed as she thought back.

"There was the driver. That man got out of the seat behind him. I think there may have been a man in the passenger seat in the front. I couldn't see for sure. No, a youth or a lady. I'm sorry. I can't really tell you"

"That's fine, Darbi. You've done well. You have given me information that we can work with. Now, we'll let Flynn or your aunt get you settled for now. We'll stay and work on this, if we may. You'll be tired of seeing us all by the time we've solved this."

"Christmas is in four weeks. Can we do it by then? Flynn needs to be able to celebrate with his aunt and uncle without danger hanging over him." Darbi refused to look at Flynn, not wanting to see rejection on his face.

"We all want that, Darbi." Flynn spoke up, his eyes not moving from her. "We want that. I want our first Christmas together to be special and danger free. Only God knows if that will happen." Flynn studied Darbi as she looked up with him, his face softening as he saw something in her eyes, something that gave him hope that he was not alone in love.

Chapter 18

Anger sparking from him the next day, Flynn stomped through the house to the kitchen. The mail that he held in his hand slammed down onto the tabletop. He was furious, to say the least. He paced around the kitchen, his eyes on the letters. Flynn reached for the top letter, the one addressed to him in bold black lettering. They were starting up again, he thought. Not what was needed.

He opened the flap, surprised to find that it was not sealed. Staring down into it, he frowned. Now what was this? He tilted the envelope to tip out the photos, hearing something metal clink on the wood tabletop. He moved aside the photos, staring at the charm that lay there. The charm, a heart shaped one, was familiar but he couldn't place where he had seen it. Sifting through the photos, he sighed. They were being followed. Some of the photos were taken of Darbi and himself in the backyard. He loved the house but suddenly decided that he would sell it and move if it meant Darbi was safe.

"God, I trust You. I know that You are here. That You hide us in the cleft of the rock and cover us with Your wings. But it is hard to trust, to see where this ends. I want to keep my sweetheart safe but I don't know how to. In a few weeks, I need to be at work and so does she. That means I can't be with her. She is already uncomfortable with my hovering even though I try not to do that. I can't help it."

Darbi thumped down the hall on her crutches, hearing the noise coming from Flynn. She wondered at that, knowing that it was not him. She worried about him, knowing that if it came to it, he would throw himself between her and danger, even if it meant his life.

"Flynn? What on earth? What happened?" Darbi rested on her crutches, her injured leg resting on the toes of that foot.

"This. They've been close enough to us to take photos of us in the backyard, among other places." He turned to her, a shuttered look coming over his face.

"Of course, they are. I wish this was over. You need to get on with your life and you can't." Darbi slid a chair back and sat, her eyes on the photos. She picked up each one, recognizing just where they had been and what they had been doing. Darbi's hands stopped as she saw the charm. "Flynn? What is this? This charm?"

"Is it yours?" Flynn sat beside her, reaching for it. He still felt that he knew whose it was.

"No, it's not." Darbi reached for it as it lay in his open hand. She turned it over. "There are initials here, Flynn."

Flynn paled, his eyes on the charm before they raise to Darbi.

"It's my mom's. The last I saw it, it was in her jewelry box." The charm dropped to the table as he was on his feet, flying up the stairs to the bedroom.

Flynn stood in front of his mother's jewelry box, hesitating before he reached to open it. It was disturbed, he could tell. He sorted through her necklaces and brooches, not finding what he was looking for. He turned his head, his eyes closing for a moment.

Walking down the steps slowly, Flynn drew in a deep breath. Darbi had turned to watch for him, a puzzled look on her face.

"Flynn?" She simply reached to hug him, drawing him down to the chair beside her. "Is it her's?"

Flynn nodded, a disturbed look on his face.

"It is, Darbi. And I have no idea when they went through it. They have been in our home. We need to have someone search it."

"If Frank were still on the case, I would talk to him. I don't know who has taken over the investigation." Darbi reached for the charm, holding it carefully. "We need to let them know."

"And we will. Just not right now. I know it's part of the investigation and evidence but it's my mom's. I can't let it go." Flynn's head went down on his arms, his shoulders shaking with his emotions.

Darbi was on her feet, crutches under her arms, as she heard a knock at the door. Richard and Silver stood there, stepping in as Darbi stood back.

"Darbi? What happened?" Richard's keen eyes studied her and then raised to the doorway. He could hear Flynn moving around.

"We got a package with photos in it. They were in our backyard watching us. And there was a charm that belonged to Flynn's mother. They were in our house, going through things." Darbi shuddered at the thought, not willing to back down any more. This was an invasion of their home and she just couldn't let it go.

Richard stared at her and then nodded as Silver moved away. He knew that she would be searching the home. He turned to the outside, looking for Stephen who was outside. A few quiet words with him and Stephen had started his search.

Darbi watched them before she moved back to the kitchen, sliding down onto her chair. Flynn had turned, his eyes shadowed as he set her mug of tea in front of her. She sighed. They needed to talk about this but wouldn't. She reached for her phone, frowning at the message that she received.

"Flynn? Where's your phone?" Darbi's quiet question had Flynn pausing as he prepared their breakfast.

Flynn dried his hands, dropping the towel on the counter, and moved to the office. He retrieved his phone, scrolling through his messages. His steps slowed as he saw the one from Joseph.

"Flynn? Did you get a message from Joseph?" Darbi's voice had his head raising before he nodded.

"I did. They were here in the house after I left. I know the security system was set. I know that I did. Someone got through it. Joseph is looking back over it, but someone had our pass code. And no-one should have had that. Only your family and my uncle and aunt have access to our home and they have their own."

Richard had approached at that point, listening to them. He had received a message from Abe, simply stating that Micah and Joseph were on their way to Flynn's home. Where was he?

"Flynn. Darbi. Abe called me." Richard stood, leaning against the counter.

"I heard from Joseph. He's on his way back here with Micah." Darbi frowned at Richard. "Someone was in our home yesterday. They used our passcodes, which they should not have had. How did they do that?"

Richard walked away, leaving them staring at one another. He pried off the cover to the security panel and sighed. It had been tampered with at some point, likely when the couple was at home and the security system not set. He snapped a photo and sent it on to Joseph. Joseph was quick to respond, simply stating that was what they had thought. Could Richard keep the couple safe for now?

Richard gave a grim laugh, knowing that would be hard to do. Someone close to them was working with their enemy. Only they had no idea who. He turned back to the kitchen, simply sitting down and then bowing his head to pray for the couple. He had work to do with them, and it would not be pleasant trying to determine who had set them up. And the shooting had been a deliberate set up to get Frank off the case.

"Who's your new investigator?" Richard's question echoed their thoughts.

"I don't know. I haven't heard as yet. Why?" Flynn turned to him.

"Because it has to be someone close to you two to have done. Not your families. We know that. That shooting was a deliberate attempt to take Frank out of the way. If it had been directed at you, Darbi, you would have been hurt a lot worse."

"That's what I figured out. Now, how do we do this? How do we trust someone new?"

"We give that person's name to Emma and she researches him or her doing what she does best."

Chapter 19

Darbi sorted through the papers set in front of her. Richard had been busy, calling in Garrett to help. Garrett worked as a private investigator and was more than willing to help. She raised her head, hearing her aunt's voice. She had not been aware that she had appeared. Darbi sighed, rising to her feet and reaching for her crutches. Darbi disappeared from the office even as she heard footsteps heading her way.

Ashlynn stood for a moment before she nodded. Darbi was hiding, something that she would do when she was worried or afraid. She would never stop that, Ashlynn decided, turning herself as she heard footsteps.

Joseph looked around the room. He and Micah had searched, finding cameras in some of the rooms in the house. He had been very disturbed at the device that Richard had found in the security keypad. That should not have happened, he knew.

"Ashlynn? Where is Darbi? I need to speak with her."

"She was here. She'll be back." Ashlynn turned, knowing that Darbi was somewhere on the main floor. She would not have attempted the stairs.

Darbi watched as Micah approached her. He had tracked her down in the laundry room where she had started a load.

"Darbi? We need to speak with you. Do you have a few moments?" He simply grinned as she scowled at him.

"You do, do you? Do I want to speak with you, though?" Darbi sighed, knowing that fear was driving her words. "I'm sorry. That wasn't very nice."

"That's okay. We've had far worse directed at us. All part and parcel of our work." Micah's hand went out to steady her for a moment. "We have confirmed what Richard and his team have found. There were some cameras in the house. The kitchen. The mud room. The living room. They avoided the office, which is strange."

"I think they were listening too closely to us. Micah, you're the computer expert. Can you search our computers?" Darbi was praying that nothing would be on them.

"I can. That was one thing that our team had decided that we needed to do."

"And what else has your team decided on?" Darbi sighed again, opened her mouth to apologize, and then snapped it closed as Micah continued to grin at her.

"It's okay, Darbi. We think differently than you do. We look at whoever it is that is in danger and try to determine where the danger is coming from. Then, we come up with plans and ideas on how to protect them. Richard is the same. I know that he and Abe have spoken. Don was in on the conversation."

"I see." Darbi slipped to a chair in front of the desk in Flynn's office. "I worry about Flynn. That he will be hurt." She shot a glance at the door. "And I feel guilty because of Frank."

"I know that you do. He won't blame you. It's his job to put himself between you and danger. It's what we all do." Micah watched her closely, seeing the strain that she was trying hard to hide from everyone. She just wasn't doing that great at hiding. "What can we do for you both?"

Darbi shrugged, her eyes on Flynn as he stood in the hallway, his eyes on her.

"I don't know, Micah. Solve this I would say." Darbi leaned into Flynn's hug, her eyes on his face. "We need this over with. We can't go on with our lives until it is."

Flynn hesitated at her words, fearing that he was losing her, that she would just move on without him.

"We can help with that. I know that Emma is trying her best to work her magic. She is waiting for information, she said, but had urgent requests that she had to work. She will not have forgotten you. Not at all."

"I see." Darbi stared past Micah. "Flynn, who is the new investigator? Do we know yet?"

"We do. It's a friend of Frank's in fact. Daniel Short."

"Daniel? Okay, I guess. He's not as good as Frank. He cuts corners. Talk to the head investigator.

———

I won't work with him." Darbi was adamant about that.

Flynn stared at her and then reached for his phone, sending off a text to the head investigator. He received a quick response which surprised him.

"Daniel has refused to work it. He's not saying why." Flynn looked at Darbi as she snorted. "Darbi?"

"He only takes the cases that are easy and makes a name for himself. Who else is suggested?"

"Adam Walker. Is he okay? He says that he went to school with Brinn,"

"He did. Yes, he's fine. He's trying to prove himself as an investigator. He's been training with Frank." Darbi looked up as Ashlynn sat beside her. "Aunt Ash?"

"He's good, Darbi. Frank has mentioned him in passing, that he is eager to learn, hunts for all the information that he needs, and then verifies everything. He's like a terrier, Frank said."

Micah began to laugh at that.

"He sounds like friends of ours. Listen, we'll be on our way. Hopefully, no one will be getting into your place again. We've strengthened it all. Your new passwords are set. Richard will check the keypad regularly for you."

"Thank you, Micah. This helps." Flynn was on his feet, walking out with Micah. He stood on the front porch, an arm around the column. His thoughts were far away from the present, returning to his past. He pondered whether something from then was playing into what was happening at present.

Timothy stopped beside him, scanning the area. He remained quiet, just waiting for Flynn to speak.

"Timothy? This may sound strange, but have we looked into Mom and Dad? Just to clear them?"

"Emma was working that way, she said. At present, she has not found anything or if she has, she hasn't said. She won't until she has confirmation of everything. That's Emma and how she works. Now, what can we do for you two?"

"For us? I'm really not sure, Timothy. I really am not. Darbi needs to heal and she won't while this is going on. She's just keeping working it until she has to sleep. Ashlynn said that Darbi won't sleep if she's working through things. And I need her to."

"Talk to your doctor. When does she go back for a followup?"

"This is Tuesday. She goes on Friday." Flynn grew pensive. "Have you heard how Frank is? I don't know his wife well enough to reach out to her."

"He's still in ICU but has roused to some extent. It was apparently looked worse than it was. He did have damage done, including to the lung, but he will heal. It will be a process, a long one at that."

"What you know about Adam Walker?" Flynn shifted until he would see Timothy's face.

A surprised look briefly crossed Timothy's face.

"Adam? He's a good friend of mine." Timothy searched Flynn's face before he nodded. "He's the new investigator. He's good. Frank has trained him and trained him well. He looks up to Frank and wants to please him. Not that he has to. He just wants to do his best for any victims that he has to work with. He knows the family and will work with you. I think his older brother, Titus, would be around your age."

"Titus? Yes, we were friends years ago. We went our separate ways once we graduated from high school. He is one person that I want to reconnect with."

"I talked with him last night. He has seen the news articles about you. He's out of town right now but said he would be in touch once he's home again."

"I look forward to that. He always challenged me to strive harder and reach farther for what I wanted to achieve. But most of all, he was an example of Christ to me. That challenged me even more."

"Yes, he's like that. So is Adam. Now, how be we head inside? You don't have a coat on, you know?" Timothy just grinned at Flynn.

"No, I don't. I didn't expect to be out here this long."

Chapter 20

Friday found Darbi restless before Flynn approached her. She was standing staring out of the window, her crutches forgotten somewhere. She had been refusing to use them and that bothered him.

"Darbi? Are you ready to go?"

"I am. Let's get this over with, please?" Darbi turned, surprised to find Flynn standing close to her.

Flynn's hands came out to grip her arms before he drew her into a hug. He just held her before he felt her arms around him, hugging him back.

"Darbi? We need to talk at some point."

"I know. I'll pack when we get back and leave." Darbi struggled to release herself, not able to do so. "Flynn?"

"We need to talk, Darbi. I am just not sure when the right time is."

"We do? And it's not?" Darbi was puzzled, sure that Flynn wanted her to leave. Only the look in his eyes said differently. "Flynn?"

"Darbi, we do need to leave. And we do need to talk. Right now, I am just so worried about you, that I'll lose you. And I don't want that to ever happen. You are the best thing in my life right now and always will be." Flynn reached for her jacket, helping her into it, and then with his arm around her, leading her from the house, locking the door behind him.

Darbi sat quietly in Jeff's cafe, her eyes on Flynn. He had seated her and then moved away to speak with Jeff, his eyes on her. It was difficult, she acknowledged to herself, coming back here. But it had been needed. She needed to do that.

Flynn slid into the booth beside her, an arm around her as she shifted over for him to do that. A puzzled look showed on her face as he just grinned at her.

"Flynn? Did the surgeon really say that?"

"He did. He is amazed at how well you have healed. It's the prayers, sweetheart. The prayers that everyone has put up on our behalf. I know he was praying as well."

Darbi grew quiet, her thoughts on her parents. She needed her mother right now. The feelings that were mixed up inside her just didn't seem to be sorting themselves out. She didn't want to talk to her aunt, even though she had never had that problem before.

"What has Adam said? I know that he has been trying to reach me, only we just keep missing one another."

"I spoke with him this morning. He wants to meet with us late this afternoon. I asked that he call before he comes over, just given your appointment this morning, which went so well." Flynn dropped a kiss on her temple, causing her to stare at him once more.

"Flynn? Did he say anything at all?"

"Not really. He's had to play catchup with the investigation. Frank isn't available for him to speak with, although he is improving. The doctors won't let him yet." Flynn thanked the waitress as she placed their meals in front of them. "And we'll find someone for you to speak with. Tag said any of his friend' ladies would." He stopped speaking as a couple hesitated beside their booth.

"Doug? Darci?" Darbi's surprise and joy at seeing them were in her voice. "What are you two doing here?"

Darci grinned, even as she slid into the booth opposite them.

"Playing tourist?" She elbowed Doug as he laughed at her.

"Flynn, this is Darci and her husband, Doug. We've talked about them." Darbi's brow lowered as she stared at them and she scowled, bringing more laughter. "You're not playing tourist. Emma sent you."

"Actually, she didn't. We just decided to come this way today. God nudged us to do that. We didn't expect to find you here." Doug shared a look with Darci. "And Darci does have information for you that we planned to drop off at your home."

"I see." Darbi leaned against Flynn, exhausted for a moment. "I need to talk with you, Darci. I need some advice."

"And I am sure that you do. I am glad to speak with you. Doug and Flynn can find something to amuse themselves while we do. Doug, you said that you needed to speak with Flynn. Emma had questions that she had no answer for and that Flynn might be able to answer."

"She did give me a list of questions. We'll talk. But for now, we'll just enjoy a meal with friends." Doug's eyes were on Darbi, seeing her discomfort. "It's hard, Darbi, going back to where you were a victim. Darci went through that, going back into her shop where she was shot. It has taken a lot of prayer for her to be comfortable there again."

"It has? Yes, I am sure that it has. I just wish this hadn't happened."

Darci shared a look with Flynn, seeing the trouble in his eyes.

"God allows good and bad in our lives, Darbi. You know that only too well. Sometimes we go through things to bring someone to justice. That's how it was for us. And for your sister and cousin. All of our friends would tell you the same thing. Now, let's set that aside for now."

Darci was as good as her words, drawing Flynn out about his work with her quiet questions. He wondered at that, realizing afterwards that as a psychologist, Darci had that ability. No one else had been able to do that with him.

Doug wandered the house inside and outside, recognizing the inherent dangers that were there but also knowing that his friends would have done their best to provide protection for them. Flynn watched him, knowing that Doug was thinking as a police officer.

Darci had sat Darbi down, her hand on the other lady's as she prayed for her.

"Darbi, what are your thoughts? What do you need to be prayed for the most?" Darci's questions were direct and to the point.

"I just feel so conflicted. I need to talk with my mom and can't." A troubled look covered her face.

"You are afraid because of the danger. You are married to a fellow who wants to take care of you and keep you safe. Only you didn't have any choice in marrying him. You are falling in love with him and aren't sure if he will ever love you. You want to move on but can't. You are having trouble trusting God in all this." Darci grinned at Darbi. "How am I doing?"

"Spot on, I would say. No one ever reads me like that." Darbi's head went back on the couch and she stared at the ceiling. "How do I do this, Darci? What advice can you give?"

"Trust God in all of this. He is there. Trust Flynn. He is in love with you, Darbi, and is afraid to speak. He's afraid that you will walk away from him. And trust your family and friends. Don't hide from them. That will cause more worry and will strain your relationship with them. Don't do that to them or to you."

"Thank you, Darci." Darbi reached to hug her. "Can I call you if I need to?"

"I expect you to. If you don't call me, I will call you. And I know that Doug will be reaching out to Flynn. You two are not alone in this. Not for one moment. Now, we need to be on our way. Read through what we have left. I reached out to the new investigator and let him have the profile. He was grateful for that. He's trying to find the ones responsible, Darbi, but they are hiding from him. That's worrying. When they are out in the open, then they can be watched. This leads me to think that there is law enforcement personnel involved."

"That's what we think, Darci." Flynn dropped down beside Darbi. "Can we pray before you two leave?"

Chapter 21

Running for his car, Flynn slid to a halt, barely able to stay on his feet. He turned and headed away from it. He didn't know the men who were leaning against it and had no desire to confront them. Pulling out his phone, he searched for messages, finding one from Darbi. It simply said that she was praying for him and to hurry home. He smiled at that. She was beginning to think of it as home, he thought.

His eyes on his car, his fingers hesitated over the keypad on his phone before he dialed the investigator.

"Adam? It's Flynn. How am I? I'm not sure. I was downtown to meet with the publisher and when I went to go back to my car, there are some men there. I don't know them." He listened for a moment before he looked around. "I've parked near the bookstore. I'll head in there."

Flynn stood near the window of the store, watching as patrol vehicles pulled in around his own vehicle. The officers exited them and approached the three men who were waiting. He could see them speaking, the officers reaching for the men's identification. One of the officers walked away, heading for the bookstore.

Shoving open the door, Flynn waited for the office to approach.

"Flynn? It's okay. They are friends, apparently, sent by other friends. You don't know them?"

Flynn shook his head.

"I don't. And with what has been going on, I'm not about to approach someone who I don't know."

"That's a wise move at any time. Come with me. I'll introduce them." The officer led Flynn back to his vehicle, his eyes moving over the area the whole time.

"Flynn.   These are friends from Riverville. Frankie Brennan. Dave Allison. Gideon Andrews. Gideon is Abe's brother-in-law. Frankie is a detective on their force. And Dave is a paramedic there. Abe felt that you and Darbi needed to speak with them, to hear their stories. They didn't mean to frighten you."

Flynn flinched at the bluntness, turning as he felt eyes on him. His focus centered on a man standing near the bookstore and he frowned. No, he thought, he didn't know him, but the man was certainly focused on him.

The officer moved away, heading for the man. He was too quick for the man to escape. A struggle ensued, bringing other officers into the fray. The three men waiting for Flynn moved to encircle him, their eyes not on him but on the area around him. This would be a perfect time for him to disappear, and they wanted to avoid that.

Frankie turned to Flynn at last, a hand out to shake his.

"I'm sorry that we surprised you. That was not our intent. Ronan knows me from what he went through. Gideon, by the way, is a private investigator. He tells me that he knows Gareth's father, Garrett."

———

117

"He does? It's a small world, then, isn't it?" Flynn's eyes narrowed and he stared at each one. "I take it that you need to speak with Darbi as well?"

"We do. Can we head that way? Gideon will ride with you." Frankie simply stared at Flynn, his face blank. He knew well have to give that look.

Flynn sighed and nodded.

"Okay. Let's head there. She's likely pacing already. I'm late getting there. I try not to worry her too much. She's been through enough in her life." Flynn reached to unlock his vehicle, not seeing the looks the three men shared with him.

Darbi turned as she felt Flynn's arms around her and hugged him back. She was growing to like this, she thought, and shouldn't. They would move on to their separate paths once this was over.

"I was worried about you, Flynn. What happened? Did your meeting run late?"

"No, it was only a short one. Everything is ready to start in January. It's just that I decided to have a bit of an adventure without you. I found three men at my vehicle, called in help, and then discovered that Abe had sent some friends to us."

"Is that what he meant?" Darbi shoved away from him, heading for her phone. "I got a sort of message from him, something about watching for some men."

"That would be right." Flynn reached for her hand, watching as she limped beside him. "You're hurting."

"I am, but not like I had been. That's getting better." She stopped in the kitchen doorway, watching the men mingling there, helping themselves to coffee. "Frankie Brennan! I might have known."

Frankie grinned at her.

"Abe said that he would let you know."

"Let me know? Do you know what he said?" She shook a finger at him as he laughed. "Your friend? Abe? You know, the one with a security team that is supposed to be so organized? All he did was send a text message telling me to watch for some men. He didn't say who." She continued to scowl at him as he laughed harder. "This isn't funny, buster."

"No, it's not. But it is. You are such a joy to know, Darbi." Frankie reached to hug her, turning her to face the other two. "This is Dave Allison. We've talked about him."

"We did. And did he bring some of Rylee's baking from her bakeshop?"

Dave grinned as he held up a box without saying a word.

"And this is Abe's brother-in-law, Gideon."

"Gideon and Rebecca. Where are your ladies?" Darbi smirked at him as she moved to make her tea. "Let's head for the office. I know that you'll need the computer. Can we solve this today and be done with it?"

"We may. There is one other thing, Darbi. Flynn had someone watching him closely. If we hadn't been there and caused him to call in patrol officers, he may well have disappeared."

"I see. Flynn, we'll talk later. But for now, what do you have for us?"

"Like that, Darbi? We will talk, but you are correct. Abe has sent them for a reason. A reason that I would very much like to know."

Chapter 22

Frankie watched Flynn carefully before his attention turned to Darbi. He had gotten to know Darbi somewhat from what Ronan and Chani had gone through. He was worried about her, to say the least, and decided that the young couple needed to get away, just to refresh themselves and have some fun. He raised his eyes to catch Dave's eye, who nodded, having the same thoughts as Frankie.

"So, Frankie, what are you thinking with this?" Flynn had been honest with the detective, sharing everything that they could.

"You have two parties involved. You have admitted that. One party is after you or Darbi. Which one of you? That we don't know but something had them bring you two together. Darbi, your family is not from here. Your aunt moved here a number of years ago, correct?"

"She did. She wanted to spread her wings as she said. She came here for college and then stayed, loving the town. She was close enough to her brothers that she could see them. We lost our grandparents when we were really young. You know the story of Dad and Uncle Adam."

"We do, and we are so sorry for that. Emma is looking into that as she can." Frankie looked at his notes, notes that he had made and notes that Emma had provided to him. "Emma is worried, to say the least. She is likely the driving force behind us being here today. She's like that. She'll mention a feeling that she has to Abe and he acts on it."

"I see. I didn't expect that to happen." Darbi reached for the papers that Gideon was handing her. "What is this?"

"Information on your family. You are aware of it, but Emma wanted you to have copies. There are enough for you to give to your sister, cousins, and aunt."

"I see." Darbi grew quiet as she read through them, her finger stopping at one point. She looked up to find Flynn watching her carefully. "This here? Where she says Uncle Adam had a run in with someone from here? What do we know about that person?"

"Not a lot." Gideon had been waiting for her to speak. "Emma's still looking into that but she said that he had contact with Flynn's parents as well. She doesn't think it has anything to do with this. Her feeling is that Flynn has made an enemy at some point, either here or out west, and that person is after him."

"I see." Darbi ignored the fact that she had just repeated herself. "How do we find out who?"

"Evan is working on that. He's devoting his time to that right now but is running into roadblocks. When I talked to him this morning, he is waiting for some information to come through." Gideon rose and paced, knowing that they were raising more questions than answering the ones already raised.

"With all this information, how do we determine who it is?" Flynn was beginning to work it as an investigation that he would do as a reporter. "I don't see that we have anything that really points to someone."

"We don't have that information yet, unfortunately, Flynn." Dave had worked with Frankie and Gideon on this. "When Rylee and I went through what we did, it was hard. It came down to the work that her father did. We helped to bring down an international crime ring. That's not likely your case. It sounds more like a revenge thing."

"Or they think that making them marry and using one against the other will make them do what they want." Gideon reached for his paperwork again, flipping through it. "That makes more sense than anything. What we need for you to do is to write down anyone and everyone that you have had contact with that made you feel uncertain and unsafe. Anyone who caused you harm that you can remember. I know it's a lot to ask and will take time. Sometimes, that is the only way that we can do this, to go back over the past. And it will likely be someone that you least expect. A friend could be doing this, pretending to be friends. Have either one of you had friends that suddenly walked away from you?"

Flynn and Darbi shared a look, neither one having thought of that possibility.

"That's a lot to ask, Gideon. Who do we give it to when we do that?" Darbi was willing to do just that, in an effort to solve this.

"To your investigator. To Emma or Evan. To one of us or one of Abe's team. We want to keep this as quiet as we can." Gideon looked around as he heard a sound from Dave. "Dave?"

"Their families need to the same. It may be someone after one of them that has done this. We've seen that before."

"We have." Frankie was on his feet, tidying his pile of notes. "Now, let us pray for you two. We need to get back on the road."

Flynn looked up late that night, realizing how late it was. He had become engrossed in the material left for them. He sighed to himself. This was not fair to Darbi, to ignore her like this. He walked through the house, turning off lights, checking that the doors were locked, and then headed up the stairs. He hesitated a moment before heading for his own bedroom. Instead, he tapped at Darbi's door and then cracked it open. The light from the hall fell across her face and he drew in a deep breath. Flynn could see the tracks of the tears that she had cried on her cheeks. He walked in and stood staring down at her before he simply laid beside her and wrapped her in his arms, a kiss on her cheek, and an I love you whispered in her ear.

Darbi shifted as she felt the arms around her and snuggled closer to Flynn. He made her feel safe, she decided in her sleep and that night, her sleep was dreamless for once. She roused in the early morning, worried for a moment as she heard someone beside her breathing. She looked around and then saw Flynn. Her face softened at that and then became worried as she thought about the danger that he was in.

Darbi was on her feet, reaching for clean clothes and then heading for a shower. Her tea started, she headed for the office, reaching for the paperwork that she had left there last night. She had grown too tired to concentrate on it and had needed that break. Today was another story. Her family would be around and they would work on it. Her phone in her hand, she sent out a group text, including Ronan, Paul and Sue, and Garrett and Meg. She paused and then added Ian and Meg, Ronan's parents. They were from this town and likely had a sense of what was going on. She frowned, thinking that they should have talked to them earlier.

Flynn roused at last, exhaustion making him sleep well past when he usually did. He rubbed at his eyes, looking around. A frown on his face, he could not understand why he was in the spare room. Then, he was on his feet, searching for Darbi. He could hear her in the kitchen and then headed back up the stairs. He had a feeling it would be a busy day and he needed a shower and clean clothes.

Darbi turned as she heard his whistle, thinking how quiet her house had been without him. Now, she waited for that sound, knowing that the one she was letting into her heart was with her and well.

"Darbi? What about your house? What are we to do with that?" Flynn simply swept her into a hug.

"My house? I'm not sure. The rent is paid until the end of the month and then my security deposit would take care of January's. I talked to my landlord,

who is Mr. O. He is not worried about that, he told me.
I was just to take what time I needed." She didn't
continue with what he had said. Mr. O had told her
that God had found her just the knight that a lady like
she needed. And he was so happy for her. If their love
was like what his had been, they were truly blessed.

Chapter 23

Ashlynn stared at Darbi that afternoon. She was not sure that she had heard her correctly.

"There was a connection here? I didn't know that." She turned and walked away, unsettled.

Darbi watched her go, feeling Brinn's arms around her.

"Darbi? Is that true?"

"Gideon and Frankie seemed to think so. They said Emma was working on that premise." Darbi looked at her cousins. "We need to work through this if we can."

"We will. Garrett is heading this way, he said, and had some information for us. And I heard that Tag was coming."

"Tag?" Darbi's eyes grew round. "Oh, my. Who all is he bringing with him?" She rubbed at her leg, feeling the pain from it that day. The stress was doing that. "We need to feed them."

"It's okay, Darbi." Paul and Sue had walked in at that point. "Jeff sent a bunch of food. No cost, he said. He wants this over for you two and this is his way of helping."

"He did? That's wonderful. Now, where do we work?"

"I suggest that we start putting paper on the walls just like everyone else has. Richard is coming by with his team. He'll work with us and keep us safe." Flynn simply reached to hug her, surprising her with a kiss to her temple. "That way, we can see it better."

"I know. I was going to suggest that very thing." She sounded disgruntled before she smirked at him, content to be held. She made no effort to move away from him.

"Okay, now that we have a plan, where do we start?" Paul looked around at the group that had gathered.

"With prayer, Uncle Paul. We need that. This is not going anywhere and we need it to." Flynn turned Darbi in his arms to face the rest.

"It's in God's timing, Flynn. Never forget that. God's timing is perfect. We, as humans, get angry and anxious and want this settled yesterday."

"You're right, Paul. That is how we do look at things." Darbi didn't continue but they knew what she meant.

Quiet conversation and questions, with the occasional burst of laughter, filled the rooms in their house. Darbi moved among them, making sure that everyone was taken care of. Peg and Meg shared a look and then moved in on her, making her rest.

Darbi sighed as they did that. She did need to rest. Her leg was paining her almost as bad as when it had happened. She had been refusing any pain medications but knew that she needed them.

Ashlynn sat beside her niece, her eyes on her. She had never expected any of her girls to go through anything but now the third one was. This was not how she had planned for them.

"Aunt Ash? When you moved here? What did Dad and Uncle Adam say?" They had talked that over before, but Darbi was grasping at straws.

"What did Aaron and Adam say? They didn't want me to move that far from home. I was their younger sister and they didn't think that they could look after me if I wasn't in their home town. It didn't matter that they were married and raising you four girls. I was still the little sister. They always looked out for me, much to my distress. I don't know that staying there would have changed anything."

"You ran away." Eilis grinned at her. "I would have too, given how those two watched out for us."

"They watched out for you, worried about you, and would have loved to see you four grow up. Your ladies are a testimony to their and your mothers' raising of you all. You had a good basis when you came to live with me. You miss them. So do I. But we have that assurance that we will see them again."

"Have you heard anything more on their investigation?" Chani was desperate to know why she had received her mother's music box. Only, no one had been able to tell her that.

"I don't know that there is anything new. I spoke with the investigator last week. Because it is that old, they are having to go back over everything and speak to the witnesses again. And some of them are not available any more for various reasons."

"This sucks, you know." Brinn's head went back as she stared up. She frowned. "Darbi, when did that decoration appear on your ceiling?"

Darbi looked up and drew in a deep breath.

"That's not a decoration, Brinn." Darbi was on her feet, limping as she walked, looking for Richard. "Richard, do you have a moment? There's something in the living room that you need to look at. And you'll need a ladder."

Richard stared at her before he followed her, looking up as she pointed. He headed for the garage, finding a ladder and also Silver.

"Silver, didn't this house get searched?"

"It did. It was done very thoroughly. Why?"

"Because there is something on the living room ceiling. I don't remember seeing it before. Has their security system been breached again?" Richard was angry.

Silver paled before she reached for her phone.

"Joseph? It's Silver. Do you have time to check the feed for Flynn's home? You do. Good. Why? Because there is something on their ceiling. Richard has headed in to see what it is."

"On their ceiling? There was nothing there when we searched the house and redid the passcodes." Joseph slid into a chair, bringing up the program that he wanted. Micah stood behind him, a hand resting on the back of his chair. "Micah? Did you get any warnings?"

"Not a one. And we have it connected so that if it was breached, there would be notification to the police force." Micah paced away and then back, reaching for Joseph's phone. "Silver, it's Micah. Ask Darbi or Flynn if anyone other than their family and friends have been in. And by friends I mean close friends. We know that Frankie, Dave, and Gideon were there."

"Hold on. I'll ask." Silver was as good as her word and back in no time at all it seemed. "Flynn said an old friend and his wife dropped by two nights ago. He was surprised to see them. He hadn't been in contact since he had moved back. I sent a text with their names and any information that you need."

"Okay, Silver. It's Joseph again. I can't see that there was anyone who got in when they shouldn't have. Even with the system off when they're home, there would be evidence on the security feed. And there just isn't."

"So we look into those friends. I sent it on to Jace and Evan as well. They'll work it as will Emma. We need to move in on them closer. The thing is that they are not ready for that."

"No, they're not. They may never be but we may have no choice in it." Joseph tucked his phone away, wanting to head for Flynn's home but not able to.

Silver waited for Richard to approach, puzzled by the look on his face.

"Richard?"

"This, Silver. It's not a camera or a listening device. I'm not quite sure what it is, but it definitely doesn't belong here. I sent pictures on to Abe to see what he can determine about it. I'm heading in to find Adam and see what he makes of it. Stay close for now. Don't let in anyone other than the ones here or Tag and his friends. Abe's on our list. We need to emphasize that. Give the others a head's up."

Silver nodded as she watched Richard drive away. She turned to find Darbi standing there. She wasn't sure how long that Darbi had been there but from the look that she was trying hard to hide, Silver suspected that she had heard Richard's words.

Chapter 24

A week passed without them being any further into finding out who it was. Christmas was coming, and Darbi despaired of celebrating it that year. Flynn had watched her and then reached for her hand. He had taken her to the attic, pulling out the Christmas decorations.

"Use what you want from here. We've brought yours over. We can combine them or buy new."

Darbi had looked at him, shocked that he would even suggest that. They had been part of their church's celebrations, although on the sidelines. They had taken part in the town's celebrations, surrounded by their family and friends. They just didn't feel safe.

"Okay, I guess." Darbi leaned against him, feeling freer to do that on her own. "Flynn, we need to talk, don't we?"

Flynn sighed. Darbi was right. Only he had prayed that this would be over and they could move on as a couple. He shifted on the floor, simply drawing her onto his knee. The attic was not a very romantic place, but given what they had been through and where they married, it was a least ten steps up from that.

"I love you, Darbi. I just wasn't sure that you would ever be ready to hear that. I don't want you to walk away and leave me. Ever. I want to grow old with you."

Darbi's eyes grew huge as she heard his words.

"You do? I didn't think that you would. I love you too. You're the knight that Mom used to weave into my stories." She gave him a sudden hard hug, feeling his hug back. "This sounds so ordinary."

Flynn broke up into laughter at that, his eyes on his sweetheart's face, seeing her consternation at her own words and then her smirk.

"It sounds cliched, but it is so true." He kissed her at that and then just sat, content to hold his love. "We need to get this over with, sweetheart. Only it doesn't seem to be going anywhere."

"Okay, so we make something happen." Darbi sat, her elbow resting on Flynn's shoulder, her eyes on the boxes stored under the low eaves of the attic. "What will your job be with the newspaper?"

"Special interest pieces. Good news stories. Stories about people who have overcome difficulties and survived." Flynn's voice slowed as he caught on to what Darbi was asking. "You want to do a story about us?"

"I do. Would he let you?"

"I can ask him." He squinted at his watch. "He'll be gone for the day but he's back in tomorrow."

"It was just a thought. Maybe it would move things along." Darbi was on her feet, heading for the stairs, a box in her arms. "Let's set up our tree, Flynn. We can start planning our story as we do so."

Flynn just shook his head. This was his Darbi, he thought. He followed her, setting down his box to shut the attic door.

Late that night, Flynn paced his office. Darbi had the right idea, he thought, knowing that they had to do something to move the investigation along. He had spoken with Adam earlier that day. That man had said that there wasn't anything right now that would move the investigation along. He had been speaking with Frank who was now at home and anxious to be back at work. Adam had a suspicion that Frank was working on this case but would never say anything.

The next morning, Flynn set his phone down. His new employer had been glad to hear from him. And he was very receptive to their idea. Jonathan had wanted to suggest something like that but had been hesitant to suggest that.

Darbi moved in on him, an arm around his neck as she perched on his chair arm.

"Flynn? How did it go? What did Jonathan have to say?"

"He wants our story, even unfinished as it is. He thinks it will be a good human interest as we are both from this town. And it will be a good lead into my position."

"I'm glad. I pray that this works. I don't think Frank would like it."

"Actually, Frank did call before I spoke with Jonathan. I asked him if it would hurt the investigation if we did something like this. He paused for a moment but said that in his opinion it wouldn't but that we should speak with Adam."

"I did speak with Adam. He's agreeable with it. He has asked that once we have it ready, we have a lawyer go over it or the PR team from the force."

Flynn was surprised at that.

"We can do that with a lawyer. I'm not sure about the PR team. They would likely want to keep things out. We will need to be very careful with what we say."

"I know. Adam and Frank would know that as well." She sighed, her head going down against his. "We'll need to speak with our families." She paused as his phone chimed.

Flynn reached for it, grinning as he read the text message.

"Emma. She wants to know when our story goes out."

"How does she do that? And have we even gone over the profile that Darci left?"

"I don't think we have and we need to. We'll do that today, sweetheart." Flynn didn't move, content to sit with his arm around her. "I guess we need to get up, don't we?"

Darbi grinned at him.

"Yes, we do at some point." She looked around his office. "You mentioned making some changes in the house. Any ideas on what?"

"Paint for one thing. New drapes or curtains, whichever you want. The floors are in great shape. The kitchen?"

"It's great. Your mom had such good taste. It doesn't look dated at all. I think new paint is all that is needed." Darbi sighed, feeling tired all of a sudden.

"You don't have to do the work, sweetheart. We'll find a painter."

"Thank you."

Flynn leaned in to kiss her and then stood, an arm around her as they wandered the house, upstairs and downstairs, talking about cosmetic changes that they would like to make.

Chapter 25

Frank walked slowly towards Flynn's home. He wanted to see the couple, not as the investigator, but as a friend. He would be healing for a long time, that much he knew. But he was very worried about them.

Darbi paused as she reached for the mail, a hand up to shadow her eyes. Yes, she thought, that is Frank.

"Frank? Are you to be up?" Darbi reached to hug him.

"I need to be. Peg dropped me off and will be along shortly. How are you?"

Darbi shrugged.

"I have no idea how I am to be. Do you?" She grinned as he shook a finger at her. "In the office, I think, Frank. Flynn's out in the backyard, doing what I have no idea. I was just about to make us a snack."

"Thank you, Darbi. Coffee sounds good." Frank stared at the paper-covered walls as he walked towards the office. He grinned. They have been busy, he thought, working with their family and friends.

"Like our handiwork, Frank?" Darbi grinned at him with the ease of old friends.

"I do. Solved it yet?" Frank took with thanks the mug of coffee offered to him and helped himself to the sweets that she was handing to him.

"We're working it. It just seems as if there is one bit of information that isn't there yet. And we need that. Or a person that we haven't found yet." Darbi bit into her brownie with an absentminded look on her face.

"That's the way it usually is. Just how are you doing though, Darbi?"

She shrugged, not sure how to answer him.

"I really don't know any more, Frank. It's a worry about Flynn. He'll be at work in three weeks, out and about and at risk. I have to start going back to the office for a few hours each week. I am not looking forward to that."

"No, you've gotten used to being at home all the time. Will you continue to work?" Frank watched her closely, nodding at Flynn as he appeared.

"I should but I am not certain that I want to continue working that job. Flynn and I have talked. We'll decide at some point what I do." Darbi looked up at Flynn, seeing his confidence in her.

"Darbi, hear me out, okay? I have a question for you." Frank set his mug down, a hand rubbing at his chest. Peg had appeared and sat nearby. "The company that you work for? How long have they been in business?"

"How long? Maybe five years. I was one of the first to go and work for them." Darbi bit at her lip, her brow furrowing as she thought through what he was asking. "We don't have a huge group of employees. Only five or six. I would have thought that we would have more than that."

"That's what our thinking is. Adam has spoken with me and asked that I talk to you. We're working together on this. I am doing what I can. We have looked into this business. It is legitimate at first look, but we're looking deeper."

"And you're not liking what you find." Flynn understood what he wasn't saying.

Frank nodded.

"That's it exactly." Frank looked around the room, seeing the changes in wall colour and ornaments that Darbi had been setting around. She was making it her home as well, slowly as it may be. "We need to ensure that the owner of this business, his partners, or other employees are not behind this. And until we have that information, we would ask that you not go into the office. We can't go in there and if we can't, then you are at risk."

Darbi had paled. Frank had just voiced what she and Flynn had talked about that morning.

"I agree, Frank. I have asked for a leave of absence for now. Until the new year at least." Darbi blew out a breath. "This is no fun, you know."

They laughed at her nonsense, knowing what she was saying.

"We'll look into them. I sent their names on to Evan as well. Emma tells me that she has some highly urgent searches that she needs to do."

"She does. I spoke with her earlier today." Darbi grew pensive, her eyes on the desk, taking in what was there. "What would you do, Frank?"

"What would I do?" Frank shared a look with Peg. They had discussed what they would have done, had it been them. "Right at the moment, we don't have a lot of information that leads us to a suspect. You are not receiving the photos and packages that a victim normally does. This tells me that they are staying very close to you, watching every time you leave the house. That's why you haven't been receiving what other victims do. They know that you are aware of how close they have been to you. They are feeding off of your fear, knowing that not sending anything will make you fear even more."

Darbi reached for Flynn's hand, finding his closing around her in a strong grip.

"That's exactly it, Frank. That is how I feel and I think how Flynn feels." She looked up at him, seeing his nod of agreement. "And we worry about the other when one is away. That doesn't help." Darbi watched Peg. "Peg?"

"I have to agree with Frank. They want you on edge all the time. That's when mistakes happen. When mistakes happen, that's their opportunity to take you again. And take you again is in their plans. It has to be."

"I am sure that it is, Peg." Flynn spoke at last, his eyes thoughtful. "I just don't see how we can avoid that."

"You can't. You could be totally surrounded and still disappear. That has happened with others. We just need to determine the best way to keep you safe. I have no idea how we do that."

"Abe's been sending me information. He's also talking to Richard. I have no idea what they are concocting, but I am sure it is something that we won't like or want to go along with." Darbi was grumbling and they all knew that. "I just want to know that my family and Flynn's are safe. Is that too much to ask?"

"No, it's not." Frank leaned forward, grimacing as he did so. "It's reasonable to ask that."

Peg spoke up at last, praying for her friends as she did so.

"It's not unreasonable as Frank has said. We want that for you. But if you can't or don't know who it is, that makes it much more difficult for us to help you."

"And we don't know that, Peg." Darbi drew in a deep breath. "You know me. You've known me for years. You know that if I had any idea of who it was, I would tell you. I don't have any inkling." Her voice died away at that, not sure how to express what she needed to say.

"Talk to us, Darbi. You've thought of something. I know you well enough to know that. Talk to us. Just tell us what you are thinking." Frank shared a look with Flynn, finding Flynn turning his attention back to his bride.

"I can do that, Frank." Darbi blinked rapidly, knowing that she had to speak, just not wanting to.

Chapter 26

Darbi began to talk, not really following what she was saying. The three with her shared many a look, Flynn rising at one point to head for the door, letting in Ashlynn and Brinn. They watched her closely, listening to the heartbreak that she had covered for so many years.

"I really don't know when it started. It was after we moved here. I never told anyone. I just couldn't. I didn't know who it was then and I don't know now. I would find small gifts on my desk at school. I would hear footsteps following me but when I looked, there wasn't anyone there. I thought I was imagining this. I would find cards and flowers on my way home with my name on them but nothing to show who they were from. I would look and then just get rid of them. They scared me. When I was in high school, they stopped to a certain extent. They have never started up again, not since I graduated from college.

"Flynn was involved, I think, somehow. I found his name on one of the cards. It was addressed to him but I didn't know who that was. I just got rid of it. I shouldn't have. I should have told someone."

Darbi's sobs broke the hearts of those in the room with her. Flynn wrapped her tight in his arms, his head on hers, tears on his own face. Ashlynn sat beside her, a hand on her back, her own heart breaking at what her niece had just confessed. *Who does this, she wondered? Who terrifies a young girl like this? And of course, she would not have told us. She would have thought that we had enough on our plates without this.*

"Darbi?" Ashlynn finally spoke.

"Aunt Ash? I didn't know that you were here." Darbi struggled to release herself from Flynn's arms and to hug her aunt.

"Oh, Darbi. I wish that you had told us. We would have looked into it then." Ashlynn looked over at Frank. "Frank, how would this play into what is going on?"

"It's possible that it does. Unfortunately, we can't say that for sure. We have no evidence of who it was. That is not helping us solve this. Darbi, we are not downplaying what you went through. We would have helped you at that point. You know that. But you were young. You had just lost your parents and were in a strange town. Other than your family, you didn't know who you could trust."

Darbi had looked at her aunt as she had spoken before her attention turned to Frank. She sighed, knowing that they were correct.

"So how do we connect that with this? And does it?"

"Do you know of anyone else that this happened to?" Frank reached for the pad and paper that Flynn handed him.

Darbi shrugged.

"There may have been. I can get you my class list and you can go through it. I know some of the girls left town as soon as they could. I often wondered why. Maybe it was because of this."

"That it might be. It doesn't explain though why there was a card with Flynn's name on it. You two didn't know each other at that time, I don't think."

"No, we didn't. Aunt Ash, would it have mattered so much?"

"It would have, Darbi. We could have helped you deal with it at the time, not have you hide it and bear that burden all the time." Ashlynn watched as Flynn rose once more, heading for the door again.

Flynn opened the door, to find Adam standing there

"Adam? I didn't expect to see you until tomorrow at least."

"God told me that I had to be here. I have some news. But you have company. I can come back." Adam stepped through into the entryway, toeing off his shoes and hanging up his coat.

"It's okay. It's Frank, Peg, and Ashlyn. Listen? Have you had your dinner yet?"

"No, actually I haven't. I was planning on grabbing something later." Adam followed Flynn to the kitchen, the light reflecting off his badge on his belt.

"Let me at least make you a roast beef sandwich. Help yourself to the coffee. You can eat here or in the office where we are all gathered."

"Here is good, thanks, Flynn. Tell me. What's going on? I don't get prompts like I did, God telling me forcefully that I need to be somewhere very often." Adam bit into the sandwich. "This is good."

"Thanks. As to what's going on? Darbi remembered something that happened when she was young, after she moved here. She would have parcels on her school desk, cards and flowers on her way home. There was even a card with my name on it once. She didn't know me at the time, so she had no idea who it was that it was meant for."

"I see. This may play into what I have found. And then again it might not." Adam's head dropped for a moment as he prayed for his new friends. "Let's go talk with the rest."

Adam sat behind the desk, watching Darbi closely. She had not heard him enter and greet the others. Her mind was taking her back to when she was young and facing that difficulty. She looked around, seeing the others watching her. She froze as she saw Adam.

"Where did you come from?" She stared at him, shock on her face.

"Your kitchen? And thank you for that delicious roast beef. Your husband offered me food, which I was thankful to receive." He grinned at her for a moment before he sobered. "Now, God told me that I had to be here tonight. Flynn let me know what you said. It may go along with what I have discovered. Frank, before we go on, can we pray?"

———

146

"We can do that, Adam. Okay, let's pray, people."

Thirty minutes later, their heads were raised, all eyes on Adam whose own eyes were on Darbi. He was not sure that she would be able to give much more information than she had.

"Okay, Darbi. Flynn said that you had mentioned what you received as a young teenager. It may relate to what information that I have been given. I have verified as much as I can. I can't tell you the source but there is word out on the street that we are looking for the men or women after you. And it could well be a woman. We all know that."

"I know that, Adam. But what can you say?" Darbi looked around, seeing the compassionate looks on the faces around her but feeling afraid of the shadows in the corners of the room that were not lit by the lights that were on.

Chapter 27

Adam nodded, knowing that Darbi need to hear what he had to say. Only he didn't think that it would help. He really didn't feel that he was that far ahead in what he was doing. And that was something that really bothered him.

"Darbi, what I have been told is very concerning. Someone is after you. And what you have just said does play into it. Apparently, this person is someone who you know and goes back to your youth. This agrees with what you told me. I don't know who, I'm sorry, but I am told that it is a male. The name has not been confirmed as yet. The person who told me this working on that. There is also a female involved."

"We figured that out. But do we have any idea why?" Darbi snuggled back against Flynn, her hand tight in her aunt's. "And is my family at risk?"

"No, we don't have information that they are other than for Flynn. And from what you related, he ties into what went on." Adam turned to Flynn. "Flynn, did you have anything happen when you were young?"

"Not that I can remember. And I would have remembered something like that. I was focused on school, my parents, my friends, and church." Flynn shook his head as he thought back to that time of his life. "No, I can't think of anything."

"That's what I thought you would say." Adam looked down at his notes. "We're working through the photos, the parcels, and the surveillance photos that we have been given. Joseph is good that way. And there have been a number."

"We thought that. We have seen evidence of the gardens being disturbed, but we couldn't tell if it was a person or an animal. Richard took a look for us and that's what he said. He indicated that you could call him."

"I'll do that. He's worked with us before." Adam finally stood, not able to provide anything more solid for them. "I'll leave but I will be in touch as soon as I have further news."

Flynn walked out with him, standing talking for a moment, not about their case but just about life in general. He watched as Adam drove away and then stood, staring up at the stars in the night sky. It was not cold, not for December. He sighed. It didn't look as if this would be over by Christmas and that was what he had been praying for.

Darbi had excused herself from the group and followed Flynn, walking towards him. She ducked under the arm that he held out, with Flynn tucking her tight to him. A kiss was dropped on her head.

"Okay, sweetheart?"

Darbi shrugged, not sure what to say.

"I'm not sure. And you?"

"Like you, I'm not sure." Flynn turned them back into the house, heading for the kitchen. "Let's get us some coffee, tea, and some snacks. We'll set this aside for now."

———

"We can do that." Darbi yawned, fatigue hitting her. She had not taken any pain medications and should have.

"Head on in and sit, sweetheart. I'll manage." Flynn watched her walk away, turning to find Ashlynn in the kitchen. "Thanks, Ashlynn. This is a big help."

"Not a problem, Flynn. You're family. It's what we do." Ashlynn shot a glance towards the hallway. "We need to help her and you but we don't want to intrude."

"You're not intruding. Darbi needs her family and to tell you the truth, I do too."

"I wish that I had known what she had gone through back then. I missed out having really good friends in Darbi and in the other ladies."

"God was not ready for you two to meet at that point. I know that you did attend the same church and youth group, but you are a little older than her. And it was a larger group, isn't it?"

"It was. We couldn't get to know everyone. There was a number there that I never did meet. I just want this over. We want to celebrate our first Christmas without this hanging over u."

"It will come, Flynn." Ashlynn's hands were busy filling the tray with mugs, the pot of coffee and tea and everything else that was needed. Flynn had been busy setting up a tray of treats and sweets to take in.

"I know." Flynn bit at his lip, staring down at the tray. Ashlynn watched him, a frown on her face.

<hr>

"Flynn? Is there something else?"

Flynn nodded, his eyes raising to stare at the photos of an angry Lake Erie and a lake freighter fighting the winds that he had hung on the wall.

"I love Darbi, Ashlynn. I told her that. And she loves me. So you can rest easy about that. We may not have planned how we married, but God did. He brought the most amazing, loving, caring person into my life, someone who I didn't know that I needed. She completes me."

Ashlynn struggled with her tears before she hugged Flynn. She turned as she heard footsteps and Peg appeared. She excused herself, leaving Peg staring after her.

"Flynn, is Ashlynn okay?"

"She is. It's just something that I said that made her emotional. Here, let's get these trays in there and enjoy some time as friends, not worrying about what is going on."

Flynn walked through the downtown area the next day, Darbi's hand tight in his. They had prayed together that morning and then looked at one another. They both realized that they were hiding and by hiding, they were prolonging their adventure. They had decided together that they wouldn't hide, not any more.

Flynn stopped at a store, his eyes on the window, before he pulled open the door and pulled Darbi with him. She protested at the store until she caught the look in his eyes and stopped.

"It's okay, Darbi. I want to do this. I have your gifts already, but you need something special." He turned to the clerk. "I would like to see your crosses, please."

Darbi had moved with him to the counter, watching as he studied them. She turned her attention to them and then simply pointed to a plain one.

"That one, Flynn. I like that one."

Flynn studied it, studied her, and then nodded. He paid for it and then fastened it around her neck. He had his mother's jewelry to give her, but he had wanted something from just him.

"Where now, love?" Darbi stared up at him, wondering at his height.

"I would like to stop at the bookstore. And then there's the candy shop." He grinned as she snorted.

"Candy? Just like a little boy." She giggled as he hugged her, a kiss to her cheek.

Chapter 28

Darbi ran for cover the next day. She could hear someone banging at her door. She grabbed for her phone and ran for the stairs, heading for the attic. She searched for the panel that Flynn had shown her, punching at it and then crawling in. Darbi pulled the door as closed as she dared before she muted her phone.

Her phone to her ear, she could faintly hear the hammering that just didn't stop. She called 911, asking for help. She waited, her breath ragged from her fear. The chiming of her phone caused her to jump and stare at it.

"Darbi? Where are you?" She could hear the fear in the frantic way that Flynn was speaking. "I'm outside but I need to know where you are. The officers will be coming in but they don't want to harm you."

"Flynn? I'm in the attic. Let me get out."

"No!" Flynn almost yelled into the phone. "Just stay put. I know where you are now. The officers are going to walk through the house and one will come and get you. He'll call you by name and tell you what your favourite flower is. That way, you'll know he's okay."

Darbi waited, barely able to breathe. Her fear increased as she heard footsteps on the stairs and the creaking as the door opened. Footsteps sounded across the floor, echoing around the room before they stopped. She heard a man say her name and that her favourite flower was a daisy. He repeated himself before she shoved open the door and peeked out at him.

The officer smiled at her and reached to help her to her feet. His hand held her steady as she stumbled and staggered, the position that she had been in stiffening her healing muscle.

"Okay, Darbi. Let's get you downstairs and to Flynn. He's very anxious, you know." He smiled at Darbi, his hand tight on hers as he led her down the two flights of stairs and to the outside. Only he took her out the back door and through a neighbour's yard before moving to the street.

Darbi was puzzled at that. She could not understand why. That was, she could not understand why until she saw the front of the house. There was just too much activity there, she thought. She watched carefully as three men were led away, their hands cuffed behind them.

"What happened?" She found Flynn who simply caught her as tight to himself as he could.

"Those men? They were sent to take you somewhere. They couldn't get in and one of them had the bright idea to bang on the door and see if you would answer."

"They don't know me very well if they think that, now do they?" Darbi sagged as her adrenaline faded. "Can I sit somewhere?"

"You can." Flynn swept her into his arms and carried her to a stretcher. "Sit here. We just need to have you checked over. Adam would want that."

Flynn shared a look with Adam, who stood outside of Darbi's line of sight.

"He would? I guess it's okay." She yawned, dropping back to lie on the stretcher. "I'm tired, Flynn. Wake me when it's morning, please." She slept, much to Flynn's amusement.

Adam approached at that, his own eyes showing amusement.

"She'll sleep for a while. I'll talk to her later. Just don't let her say anything to anyone. I've cleared it for you to travel with her. Off you go."

Flynn paced the room while waiting for Darbi to awaken. It didn't seem as if that would happen any time soon. She had roused slightly as she was shifted from the stretcher to a bed, before she slept again. She needed it, he knew. Flynn just wanted her awake, to talk with him, and assure him that she was okay.

Ashlynn and Brinn had appeared, assessed them both and left, promising to come back. He had heard from Chani and Eilis, simply telling them that Darbi was sleeping and that she couldn't tell them what had happened, not until she spoke with Adam. And he had no idea when that would be.

Darbi roused in the early morning, not sure where she was. She was afraid, she decided, more afraid than she had been. Only, she didn't know why. She didn't think that she was blocking anything but she was no longer sure. Darbi decided that she needed to speak with Darci at some point that day. Flynn would help her with that, she knew.

———

Flynn roused as he heard soft muttering and a smile crossed his face. Darbi was awake and telling herself off by the sounds of it. He rose from the uncomfortable chair that he had slept in and simply reached for his bride.

Darbi jumped and then clung to him, not sobbing as he expected. She was angry, he decided, and rightly so. This had been brought back to their home and he hated that for her.

"Darbi? You spoke with Adam?"

"I did. He was around late last night, I think when you were out getting something to eat or your coffee. I could barely stay awake. I don't know the men. Who were they?"

"Adam said they were muscle for hire and from out of town. He's trying to track down who hired them but they aren't talking." He grinned at her snort. "About what you expected?"

"Of course it is. When can I leave here?"

"Now, if you like. Brinn stopped at our place and found some clean clothes for you. The officers were still there and let her in."

"I don't get it, Flynn. Why the house? Would it not make more sense to try and take me when I'm out and about?"

"You haven't been. You are staying very close to home. They had to take a chance to nab you. You did well to run and hide as you did." He grinned at her. "I used to hide in there when I was a kid. Mom would pack me a snack, hand me a flashlight and a book, and then tell me to go and hide from the latest villain in my book. She made life an adventure."

"I would have liked to have known her." Darbi reached for her shoes, pulling them on and then opening the curtain. "I can really leave?"

"You can. Here, let me take the bag. Richard is waiting for us."

"Richard? Of course, he is. And he won't let me out of his team's sight. I just know that." Darbi was grumbling again.

Richard stood behind her, a grin on his face. Naomi was openly laughing.

"She's about right, isn't she, Richard?" Naomi moved forward, to hug Darbi. "You knew that we were there."

"I did." Darbi smirked at Richard, who continued to grin at her.

"Let's get you home, Darbi. I'm driving. Flynn doesn't have a vehicle here." Richard pointed towards the elevator.

Darbi moved that way, her hand tight in Flynn's. She saw Richard's three team members surrounding her and realized that Stephen must be in the vehicle. How Richard knew when to come, she never did understand. And she never did ask him.

"Okay, Darbi. We'll get you home. We've gone through your home. Nothing was disturbed. They didn't make it in through your door." Richard turned to look at her.

"I know. I just wish this was over." Darbi's head went down on Flynn's shoulder. "I am getting so angry."

"Anger works. God doesn't tell us that we can't be angry. It's what we do with it that counts." Richard had surprised her with his words. "We need to let God have control of our anger. We can't use it to hurt someone or do something wrong. Your anger can help drive you to find the ones responsible. That is one way that you can use it."

Darbi nodded, knowing that he was correct. She had never thought of it that way and should have, she knew. *Okay, Lord, where do we go from here? How do we find these people? They are hiding in plain sight. Yesterday shows that. And I want to find them. Only I'm scared that they will go after Flynn, my family, his family, and our friends. I don't want anyone hurt. And I don't see how we can avoid that.*

Chapter 29

Three weeks passed. Christmas came and went. Flynn had watched Darbi with her family and appreciated how much she was trying. He himself had felt welcomed to their circle. He watched around the house and around them every time that they were out. Flynn worried about Darbi each time she was away from him. He prayed for peace about what they were going through and found it at times. He knew that God was there in everything but was still finding it hard to trust.

The new year arrived and with it more worry for both Flynn and Darbi. She knew that he would be at work and out in the community. The ones after them had been quiet for a few weeks, leaving Darbi to hope that they had given up on them. Flynn had simply shaken his head, knowing that they hadn't

Their plan to put out a piece in the paper had been taken from their hands. Jonathan, the publisher, had listened to their plans a few days before Flynn started work. He had sat back, his eyes on his hands before he looked up at them.

"Here's what we do, Flynn and Darbi. We do a piece welcoming you to our publishing family. A special interest piece. Then we tie it to an updated piece detailing what we can of the investigation. We have been following it all along, just not printing much about it. Now that you're part of our family, we will push it. Flynn, for now we'll keep you in the office as much as we can. There will be times that you do need to be out there. At those times, we will have someone with you." Jonathan's hand went up at the protest put forward. "We have had officers volunteer to do that. These volunteers are in law enforcement."

"There are? I didn't know that." Flynn had shifted in his chair, his eyes on Jonathan before he looked at Darbi, finding her nodding.

"That works, Jonathan. Now, can we contribute to the welcoming piece?" She had grinned at Jonathan, finding him grinning at her in return.

"That you can. Darryl is waiting for you to do just that." Jonathan was on his feet, his eyes on Flynn. "Flynn, I was friends with your father and am friends as well with your uncle. It is good to see you back home. This is not the welcome that we would want, though."

"No, it's not, but it is what it is. God has allowed it for some reason." Flynn reached for Darbi's hand, following Jonathan as he headed for Darryl.

A hand crumpled the newspaper two days later. The man was enraged, storming around his office. They had not named him. He didn't think that they had that but now? He wasn't sure. They seemed to have too much information that would lead to him. He stared down at the newspaper that he had crumpled and dropped to the floor. His foot came out and he stomped on it. That's what he would do, he decided. He would find them and stomp them to pieces. Only he had to do it in such a way that no one ever found out.

He turned and his hand reached for his phone. A number dialed, a few words exchanged, and he replaced the receiver carefully. His plans were now in place. And he had no doubt that they would be followed through on. Time was not on their side, he thought. He would take care of them.

Darbi shivered as she walked through the grocery store that afternoon, carefully placing the items that were on her list into it. She paused, her eyes searching the store. She had such a sense of danger and being followed. She could not shake it that morning.

Silver watched her and then the area around her. Richard had received word that someone else was looking for them and had every intention of finding them. He was at a loss as to who it was. And Silver knew that was not him.

"Darbi? How's the shopping going?" Silver grinned at the lady who she was now considering a friend.

"Silver? My shopping? I just need.." Darbi's voice died away as she looked down at her list and then into her cart. "Did I really need all this?"

Silver began to laugh, with Darbi joining in after a moment.

"It's different shopping for two, isn't it?" Silver tilted Darbi's hand to read her list. "Okay, just some juice and your tea and coffee. That should do it. Let's roll, Darbi. I want to do something fun this afternoon."

"Do something fun? And just what would that be?" Darbi stood in line, watching the customers around her. She nodded at acquaintances and friends.

"I don't know. We need to come up with something. Are you working now?"

Darbi shook her head.

"No, I'm not. Flynn and I decided that I wouldn't. I'll look for something soon, but at the present, I just feel that I am too dangerous to be in an office. Does that make sense?"

"Perfect sense." Silver waited as Darbi paid and then walked with her to her car. "Okay, let's get these home and put away."

Darbi turned from her fridge, an eye on the clock. It would soon be afternoon and she would need to decide on that night's supper.

"Okay, Silver, what was it you wanted to do?"

Silver had searched through the house as Darbi had been busy. She noted that the paper had been removed from the walls.

"Where does your research lie?"

"Our research? About there. Why? You're wanting to work on it?"

Silver nodded, assessing Darbi as she did so. She saw the fear and pain that she was trying to hide.

"Don't hide how you're feeling from me, Darbi. I've seen more than I ever thought I would. But I am where God wants me. That's what counts."

"It does, doesn't it?" Darbi perched in the desk chair, reaching to wake up the computer. "I hate this but I know God is allowing it. I know too that He is in control and wants only the best for us. It's up to me to follow Him and trust Him."

"That's the hard part, Darbi. To trust God in situations where you have no control." Silver sat near her, her eyes on her friend. "Now, where is the investigation? Has Adam talked to you lately? And have you had anything else come to you?"

"All those questions!" Darbi laughed at Silver, not realizing that had been Silver's goal, to make her laugh. "No, we haven't had anything. Adam was around two days ago. He's had to set it aside, he said. With no new evidence or new threats, he can't devote time to it like he wants to."

"Okay, so then, it's up to us. A friend of ours was around last night, just asking what was going on."

"A friend? Do I know that person?" Darbi watched as Silver hesitated. "It's okay, Silver, if you can't say who."

"It's not that. It's just who it is." Silver reached for Darbi's hands, bending her head to petition God for a resolution to this that they were under. She raised her head at last, her eyes thoughtful. "He says that he knows you but didn't want to approach you directly."

"That is bizarre, Silver. Who is it?"

"Jacob Whitson. From Mistletoe. Do you know him?"

"Jacob? I do. I know his wife, Finn, better. What would bring him to come to you?"

"That was puzzling. He just said that he had been very burdened for you. A friend's father did some research when he heard your name and came up with some things. I have that all in the folder on your kitchen table. Read it through, discuss it with Flynn, and then come see us. Adam has been given a copy."

Silver rose to her feet, her eyes on the window across from her. She could see the bare branches just waiting for spring to leaf out. She prayed for her friend, desperate to know that this couple would survive to see spring.

Chapter 30

Flynn walked slowly into the house that night. He was exhausted from the day. There had been a bomb scare at the newspaper office which had turned out to be a false alarm. Still, it had sent them scrambling to get the paper ready for printing for the next morning.

He sniffed the air, liking the aroma of roasting chicken and baking potatoes. He hadn't replied how much he had missed coming home to meals ready to eat. He knew that it would't last, that at some point, Darbi would find work.

Darbi turned, a smile on her face, and walked into his arms. She hugged him tight, feeling the tension in him, but also needing to talk with him about what Jacob had sent.

"Okay, love?" She leaned back to look up at him.

"I am now that I'm home. Something happened today that I need to discuss with you. Do I have time to change before we eat?" He reached to kiss her, watching her blush as he did so.

"You do. It will be about thirty minutes or so. I didn't get it in the oven when I planned." Darbi bit at her lip, uncertain as to that.

"It's okay, sweetheart. It's okay. I don't care what time we eat. All I care about is that you are here with me."

Their dinner over, Flynn reached to snuggle Darbi close to him. She had headed for the living room, her eyes on the folder that she had placed on the table there.

"Darbi? What happened today? I know something did."

"There was. But what happened with you?" Darbi shifted to look up at him.

"There was a bomb scare at the office. It wasn't anything and we don't know why. We had to scramble, all of us, to get the paper ready for printing."

"Related to us, do you think?"

"We don't now. Jonathan says that they get this regularly. It is usually a case of someone being upset with a news article." Flynn stretched out his legs, not wanting to move. "So what happened today?"

"Silver was with me when I went shopping. She came back here. When we were talking, she said a friend had gone to them. I didn't know that. He had information from a friend's father that he wanted them to look at. And yes, Adam has been given a copy."

"And who is the friend?"

"Jacob Whitson. From Mistletoe. I know his wife, Finn, better. We connected through a conference a couple of years ago."

"I see." Flynn reached for the folder. "And this is what he gave them?"

"It is. I looked through it. I just don't see the connection." Darbi leaned against Flynn as he opened the folder and began to read.

Flynn set the folder aside, troubled by what he had read. Those very names had just been suggested to him today by a fellow reporter who had been a close friend in his youth.

"I'm not surprised at the names, sweetheart. They were mentioned to me today in fact."

"They were? So, where does that leave us and what do we do?" Darbi chewed at her lip as she thought through what they could do. "We need to go on the offensive, Flynn."

Flynn laughed at her ferocity.

"And just how do we do that?"

"We planned to be out and about more. We haven't done that. It's not that we couldn't. It's that we chose not to. Aunt Ash mentioned that last night when we were speaking. We're hiding."

"That's exactly what we have done. Staring tomorrow, we change that. It's Saturday. We're going out for breakfast, walk the downtown. Spend time with our families. And Sunday, we're at church and then out for lunch with everyone. Does that work?"

"It does. And you will be out and about with your work. I need to find something to do. Brinn asked if I wanted to work for her for now. She's finding more and more clients with her petsitting business."

"And how do you feel about that?"

Darbi shrugged, not sure.

"I don't know. I love animals but I'm not that much into taking care of others. Maybe I should go back to the transcription office."

"But you don't want to."

"No, I don't. I was finding that I didn't enjoy it as much anymore. And hearing that it had only started up around the time I graduated and was looking for work makes me think that something was off about it."

"There is that. Don't rush, sweetheart. We're okay if you don't work, but I know that you need to. How about hobbies? Any particular one that you want to try?"

Darbi shrugged, her head going down on Flynn. Her eyes closed as she slept. Flynn tilted his head to watch her before he reached for his phone. He hesitated as he prayed for her, the love of his life, and he didn't want to lose her. Not yet, anyway.

He leafed back through the papers, stopping at the first page again. It was a summary of what had been determined. This man is good, he thought, before he set it aside, his own eyes closing as he thought through the day. It had been a stressful one, there was no doubt on that. Now, how did they continue to live their lives?

Lord, he prayed, *I can't do this anymore. I can't keep my lady safe. I feel like we are in the middle of a hurricane of some sort and we may not survive. I yield to Your plan, but it's still hard. This is something that I need to do over and over, yielding to You. Please, dear Lord, protect my precious and beloved Darbi. If anyone has to die, let it be me.*

The couple slept, not hearing the sounds of the wind as it picked up. The wind hid the sounds of people moving around outside their house. Flynn had wondered long afterward if it would have made a difference to what they faced if they had heard the men. No one could tell him that for sure.

Chapter 31

Darbi held onto Flynn's hand tightly the next morning as they walked through the downtown area. He was as good as his word from the previous night. He had taken her out for breakfast and then willingly walked through stores with her. Not that they were purchasing anything, Darbi thought. It was nice to be out and about once more. She had missed that freedom.

Flynn groaned as his phone chimed. He pulled it out, staring at the message that he had received.

Darbi stared at him and then at his phone. Her face showed her shock.

"Flynn? What is this? What does this mean?"

"It means that we are in trouble and real danger, sweetheart." Flynn looked around, pulling her with him as he ran for his vehicle. He shoved her inside and then headed for the police detachment.

"Stay here. Keep the doors locked." Flynn was out of the car, leaving the keys with Darbi, just in case. He headed for the desk officer, who looked up in surprise.

"Flynn? You're here?"

"I am. Is Adam in?"

"No, he's not. He's off this weekend and away he said. What can we help you with?"

Flynn hesitated, his phone in his hand.

"I have a message that I need to get to someone. It's threatening us and I don't like it."

The officer reached for Flynn's phone and studied the message before he forwarded it to the lab.

"I've sent it to the lab. I'll also send Adam a message about it. The lab will search it through to see if they can determine where it came from."

"Thank you. I'm heading home with Darbi. We had planned something else for the day." Flynn paused, a thought disturbing him. "Can I have a patrol officer swing by and look the house over? This message may have been a ruse to get us out of the house. That's what it seems like."

"We can do that." The officer moved away and then was back to Flynn. "Head on home, Flynn. Someone will be there by the time that you get there."

"Thank you." Flynn headed back to his vehicle, his eyes on Darbi as her head turned. She was uneasy, he could tell, and afraid. An officer stopped beside him, a hand on his arm.

"Flynn, get your wife out of your vehicle. Now. We need to search it."

Flynn stared at him, shock on his face before he spun to stare at his car. He felt the officer's hand shove him from behind before he ran for the car. He banged on the window, frightening Darbi who stared at him in horror. He frantically pulled at the door handle with both hands, all the while calling for Darbi to open the door. She fumbled for the lock, finally able to push the right button. She reached for Flynn's hand as he moved in a frantic motion to pull her from the car and run with her. Her purse flew from her hand as she ran with him, not knowing why.

The sudden eruption of noise and fire flung them forward to the ground. They laid in a sprawled heap, the officer beside them, not moving. Shouts and calls for help rang through the mid-winter, mid-day air that had silenced with the noise. Flames shot into the air, preventing anyone from approaching the car.

The officer moved, raising himself to his elbow, his eyes on the car and then on the couple before he was on his knees. Flynn began to move himself, disoriented by the explosion. His head raised and then dropped back down as his eyes closed. His ears rang from the noise, enough that he could not understand what was being said to him.

Darbi didn't move, her eyes closed. She didn't feel the hands on her, assessing where and how badly she was injured. She didn't respond to the calls for her to come around.

The paramedics moved in even as the firefighters worked on the car. Paul stood for a moment, staring at the car and then around him before he ran for the group gathered around the young couple. A hand on an officer's shoulder, he stopped, a sound torn from him

"Flynn? Darbi? They're alive?"

"They are, Paul." He was drawn back from the scene a few feet. "Let the guys work on them. You need to work your crew."

Paul was torn, knowing that he was indeed needed at the fire scene, but wanting to be with his only nephew. He turned, finding his assistant captain moving in.

"Paul?" Jeff spoke to him, waiting for him to respond. "It's Flynn?"

"It is. Do we know what happened?" Paul turned back to his job, intent on finding out why the car was on fire.

"It exploded from what we can tell." Jeff watched as the crew worked to extinguish the fire. "It will take a while for the investigation to work. How's Flynn?"

"I don't know. He and Darbi are alive, thank God for that."

"Yes, that's true. Listen, once we have this contained, head over to the hospital. I spoke with the chief and he wants you there."

"Thanks, Jeff. Let's see what we can find out now. They're in good hands."

Ashlynn stood at her desk, her eyes on her employer. She was working a rare Saturday, just to help get the office back into shape after the Christmas closure. Her head began to shake.

"It can't be. It must be someone else." She sank against her desk, frantic to hear that it wasn't Darbi and Flynn.

"I'm sorry, Ashlynn. They have been injured." He watched with compassion as she nodded and then reached for her jacket and purse. "There's an officer here to speak with you. He'll drive you to the hospital. We don't want you driving on your own. Don't worry about your work." He sighed and smiled slightly as Ashlynn tidied away what she had been working on.

Ashlynn walked rapidly into the Emergency Department to speak with the clerk and then turned, looking for who she just wasn't sure. She saw a fire turnout coat in her peripheral vision and looked up.

"Paul? You're here?"

"I am. I worked the scene and then was sent here. Sue's on her way in. I took the liberty of calling your girls. They were scattered today, they all told me, some out of town, but they were heading this way."

"They were. It's not something that we normally do but with the girls married or engaged, that's what has been happening. I was at work." Ashlynn shrugged out of her jacket. "What can you tell me?"

"Flynn's car exploded. No, they weren't in it. Thank the good Lord for that." He looked up as Sue found him. "I don't know much more than that."

"God has His hand on them. He has all along. We just need to find out who is behind this." Ashlynn kept shifting on her chair, not able to sit quietly.

"And we will. This? This happened in front of the police station. One of the officers was injured as well."

"They are bold, aren't they? But it is was a bomb, it could have been planted at any time and remotely detonated. At least that's what I think."

"It could have been, Ashlynn." Paul looked up as he heard a sob and moved to let Eilis have his chair.

"Aunt Ash? What happened? Paul didn't say much, only that I needed to come." She hugged her aunt, tears on her face.

"Darbi was hurt, love. I don't know how bad yet." Ashlynn watched her niece, knowing how this was tearing the girls apart to have each one going through something. She prayed for her nieces and their partners and for the one niece who was still single. She didn't think to pray for herself.

Chapter 32

Darbi roused, turning to her side and fighting the nausea that threatened to overwhelm her. She closed her eyes again, willing the vertigo to stop. She opened them again, to stare at the medical equipment in front of her.

Not again, she thought. *Not again.* Who did what this time? She raised her head, looking around before she shoved back the sheet and shifted to sit on the side of the bed. She was on her feet, moving for the door, looking back at the bed for a moment.

She walked through the hallway, not finding anyone to stop her before she headed for the outside door. A hand stopped her, causing her to jump and give a small scream.

Adam watched her closely. He had been waiting for Darbi to awaken so that he could talk with her and find out her side of what happened. He just hadn't expected to have to stop her. His hand directed her to a chair where he shoved her down and then sat in front of her.

"Darbi?"

Darbi squinted against the light.

"Adam? What are you doing here? It's the middle of the night, isn't it?"

Adam gave a grim smile.

"It is. And you are the reason I'm here. I need to talk with you about what happened."

Darbi thought about shaking her head at him and then had a second thought. That would be too painful, she decided.

"I don't know why I'm here. Do you? And just why are you here? I don't need the police. At least, I don't think that I do."

"I am here because you do need the police and have for a number of weeks. As to what happened, Flynn pulled you from his car before it exploded." Adam raised his eyes to see Flynn standing nearby, his eyes on Darbi.

Flynn moved to sit beside her, a hand reaching for hers. He found that she jumped as he did that, her eyes huge as she stared at him.

"Who are you?" Darbi could barely get the words out.

Flynn nodded at Adam, having expected questions like this. The physician had spoken to him and to Darbi's family at his request.

"I'm Flynn. And look at your hand. You're my bride."

Darbi stared at him in shock and then down at her hand.

"I'm sorry. I don't remember." She kept staring at her hand, before she sighed. It was coming back in bits and pieces. "What did they do to the car, Flynn? They had to do something. You pulled me from it."

"I did, sweetheart. We almost didn't make it in time. Can you tell Adam anything about what happened while I was inside?"

"Nothing. I didn't see anything at all and I was watching. When did they do this? And was it a bomb and not something wrong with the car?"

"It was a bomb." Adam's words brought her around to face him. "We have determined that. Thankfully, you were not hurt seriously. All three of you could have been killed. And that was the plan."

"If we're dead, who wins? Who hates us this badly that they want that?" Darbi turned from Adam to Flynn and back again.

"That we don't know yet. There was not a lot of evidence left on the car. However, your home is another story."

"Our home?" Flynn wasn't sure what Adam meant.

"Your home. We have to take you somewhere else to live for now. You will be escorted in to get what you need for the next couple of weeks and then you will need to go elsewhere. We have a security team moving in to protect you."

"Richard?"

"No, Don. He's from another town close to here. He has five men who work for him." Adam stood, staring down at them. "This is no longer an option, Darbi, Flynn. Whoever is it? They could very easily have killed you. If the officer had not asked you about your car, Flynn, you would have just gotten back in and driven away. That would have killed you both. Now, come with me. I'll take you to your place and wait for you to pack."

Darbi stared at their home, seeing the crime scene tape that floated in the light wind that was blowing in the early morning. She sighed to herself. Now, where were they to go? She could see six men milling around that she didn't know.

Flynn stood, his arms around his bride, waiting for someone to tell them that it was okay to go in. He was afraid, he knew and that meant he grew angry. He didn't like that at all.

Adam walked back towards them, Don beside him. He didn't know the couple but would get to know them over the next few weeks. Richard had been upfront with him, telling him what he could of Flynn and Darbi. Don had nodded, knowing that Richard would have stepped in if he hadn't already had a commitment.

"Flynn? Darbi? This is Don. He's going to be with you for the next few weeks. Listen to what he says. It may be the difference between your life and death or that of your families."

Darbi stared at him, a mutinous look on her face. Don just stared back.

"I won't be separated from my family. I just can't."

"We understand that, Darbi. I promise that you can speak with them and we will get you together with them at least once a week. It's the best that we can do. But whoever this is may use them to get to you."

"We understand that, Don. But it's not an option. Darbi has contact with her family. That is not an option." Flynn stared at Don, not backing down.

Don nodded. Richard had warned him that this would be the response. And that at some point, Darbi's whole family would descend on them to work through who was after them. That's what they did. Don had nodded, knowing that was true. He would manage it. He always did.

"Okay, we walk you in. You pack what you need. Your phones are left here. So are your computers. We don't take anything that can be tracked. Your shoes? We will check them for tracking devices. That's what we do, folks. Now, let us get you in and out. We want to be away before light breaks. And we will apologize to your neighbours for disturbing them so early in the morning."

Don watched as the couple moved towards their home, four of his men with them. Paul stood beside him, his eyes searching the darkness.

"I don't like this, Don. Someone is out there."

"There is. There always is. We just need to take every precaution that we can. We'll separate them into two vehicles to leave. That's not going to go over well."

"No, it won't."

Chapter 33

Darbi paced the living room of the house that they had been taken to. It was still in her town but she was not familiar with the area. It was on the other side of town, a more rundown area. She wondered at that but had then shrugged. Don seemed to know what he was doing. If Richard was his friend, then he must be okay. She turned to watch two of his men who were standing in the hallway, deep in discussion. Darbi thought that their names were Paul and Thomas but she wasn't sure.

Flynn had approached her, stepping in beside her, an arm around her. This was not what they needed or wanted. Not at all, he decided, but they had no option. If they didn't do this, they might now live. The only thing that he had asked was that he still work. Don had nodded, having already thought of that and spoken with Jonathan. Jonathan had been shocked to hear of the explosion, not realizing that it had been Flynn's car.

"How are you, sweetheart?"

Darbi shrugged, not sure how she was.

"All right, I guess. I don't like this."

"I know that you don't. Neither do I. We don't have much of an option, I don't think."

"No, we don't. Did we bring all the paperwork with us that we were working on?" Darbi looked around, not sure where anything was.

"We did. And we will work on it. Today, we rest."

"No, I can't. I need my aunt and my sister and my cousins." Darbi burrowed against Flynn as she began to weep, her sobs breaking his heart.

Flynn swept her into his arms and looked around, finding a chair to sit. He cuddled her close, his prayer whispering in her ear. He felt her relax and sleep. Flynn nodded as Paul dropped a blanket over Darbi before he moved away.

Paul stood for a moment, staring at the couple before he turned to Don.

"What is actually going on, Don? Who tried to kill them?"

"No one knows for sure. Listen, we need to meet as a team. Find the rest. Thomas, I know, is in the kitchen, sorting through our meals."

"Will we be able to stay here for a while or will we be on the move?"

"I pray that we can stay here for a while, but there's no guarantee of that. There never is."

Don looked around at his team. Each one had their own specialty and personality but they worked together as a team, as a unit. That would be needed.

"Okay, fellows. We're here with Flynn and Darbi. I don't know who is after them. That is not clear to anyone as yet. Flynn did say that he had paperwork they have been working through. We'll do that with him as we can. Pray that we can stay here for a while. We all know that may change in a moment."

<hr>

Thomas nodded, knowing that was true.

"I'll take on the meal prep, Don, as always. Darbi may want to do that as well, just for something to do."

"And Flynn will be working, you said?" This came from Joshua.

"He will be. Remotely for now. I spoke with Jonathan. He's willing to do what he can to help us out. If needed, Flynn goes on leave or just does guest columns for them." Don rubbed at his head. "This is difficult, fellows. We don't know who it is and that means it could be anyone."

"Who's running the investigation?" Caleb shared a look with the other men.

"Adam is. Frank had been until he was shot. He's not quite cleared to come back to work yet, but he has been working on the case as he can with Adam."

"Good. Both are excellent investigators." Mark turned away for a moment, squinting at his phone. "I got the report from their home. It was worse than we thought."

Don stared at him before he sighed.

"How bad?"

"Numerous bombs set around. Cameras all over the place. Tracking devices on their footwear. Someone wanted to keep track of them and didn't care how."

"The bombs would have sent them running, and that would have meant they ran right into the culprits' hands." Don rose and began to pace. "We need to make plans, fellows, more than one. If it means that we split them up, then we do."

"And they will fight us on that." Mark rose and headed for the office door and stood to watch Flynn pacing. "They're already restless."

"They will be and it will only get worse. Come up with our plans, fellows, and we'll collate them. Next meeting tonight." Don walked away to head for his vehicle. He needed to talk with Adam and that he wanted to do in person.

Adam looked around as he heard his name called and waved. He grabbed his cup of coffee and the extra one that he had asked for and walked towards Frank. Don appeared beside him.

Frank waited for Adam or Don to speak, knowing they were meeting for a reason. That reason bothered him greatly. He had been shocked when he heard about Flynn's car, not knowing how to respond to Ashlynn and the girls as they had faced him. They had asked for his advice and he gave them what he could.

"Don? They're safe?" Adam finally asked the question that had been uppermost in his mind.

"For now they are. But we can't promise they will stay that way. You know only too well how it works."

"We do. What can we do to help?" Adam reached for his notepad and pen.

"We need to solve this and solve this yesterday. That's the main way that you can help. Other than that, feed us the information that we need as you can. Anyone who is confirmed as a suspect? We need to know that if you can release that information. We can't work blind." Don sipped at his coffee, his eyes on the other two men.

"We can do that. I'm back in the office on Monday and will make this case a priority, working with Adam. I can't be out in the field as yet." Frank was frustrated and it showed.

"And that will help, Frank. You have experience and resources that I don't and may never have." Adam leaned forward, deep in thought. "I don't understand though why someone is after one of them. We still haven't gotten a clear picture on that."

Frank nodded, having had a lot of time to mull that over. He simply spoke his thoughts, leaving the men to stare at him and then one another. Don began to nod, knowing that Frank had read the situation the same way that he had. And Adam was heading that way.

"We'll work on that, Don. And if I read Flynn rightly, if he's come up with that name, he'll be researching it. Has anyone heard from Emma?"

Don nodded.

"I did. I reached out to Abe just to let him know what was going on and to ask for help if we needed it. They've been away and Emma has not had a chance to work on it. And her employees haven't either. She's changing that now to make this a priority for herself.

She thinks that she'll have some information today. Abe was dismayed to hear what had happened."

"And she will come through. Adam, you can expect to start receiving information from her today. And it will be just what you need to follow the trail to the culprit and arrest them." Frank grinned at Adam.

"I will? I have heard of her. The other investigators have talked. I can't wait." Adam grinned at them, not realizing the volume of data that Emma would indeed send him.

Chapter 34

Darbi looked around from the computer that she had been using. Thomas had set her up and stayed close as she worked, ready to answer any questions that she had. She was puzzled, that was an understatement.

"Thomas, can you take a look at this? I think I figured out who it is." Darbi moved away from the computer to let Thomas sit there.

Thomas studied her before he looked at the screen. His eyes narrowed as he scrolled through her notes. *She's good,* he thought. *She's found the one who we have been looking for.*

"Thomas?" Darbi could barely speak, hope evident in her voice

"You're good, Darbi. This is who it is. We need to get this to Adam. He'll verify your information and then hopefully we can get you home in short order."

Darbi's face lit up as she grinned.

"Really? I'm glad." She felt arms around her and leaned back against Flynn.

"Darbi? What have you been up to?"

"Solved this, I think. Take a look." Darbi beamed at him.

"Solved it, have you?" Flynn took a look at the work on the computer, sharing a look with Thomas who was grinning at them.

Don had appeared, wanting to know what had happened. He nodded as he listened, reaching for the pages that Thomas was printing. He read through them, a frown on his face as he saw the name that Darbi had narrowed it down to. He nodded, his eyes on Darbi, who was staring back at him.

"Don? What are your thoughts?"

"You're good, Darbi. Tell you what. You're looking for work. I'll hire you and send you for training. You can do research for us." Don grinned at the stunned look that covered her face before she was on her feet hugging him. "Now, let me find someone to head off with this. They'll find Adam or Frank."

"Can I talk with my family, Don? I need that. We usually talk every couple of days and haven't." Darbi felt as if she was begging.

"We can do that for you, Darbi. First, our lunch and then we'll see about your family. It's Saturday. Will they be around?"

"They should be. They usually are on Saturdays." Darbi bit at her lip, missing her family greatly. "I just need to talk with them. They need me. And I need them."

"We know that you do." He pointed to the kitchen, before he headed to find Caleb and Mark, sending them on their way. He walked away, praying that Darbi had indeed been correct. He had no doubt that this person was involved. He squinted at his phone as it rang. "Abe?"

"Don? Where are you?" Abe's voice was rushed.

"Still in the house that we were in."

"Get out of there and now. You've been found. We're on our way to you."

Don spun, running back for the house, shouting for them to gather what they could and head for the vehicles. The team scrambled, rushing to do that. Flynn and Darbi flew to do the same, heading for the vehicle that sat ready to leave.

Don looked around as Paul sped away, seeing the vehicles that were heading their way. Thank you, Lord. Abe called at the right time. His phone was out as he called Adam, simply telling him that their safe house had been found.

Adam stared at the phone in consternation and then at the two men sitting across from him.

"That was Don. He had to run."

"That's what we have been expecting. To have to leave there." Caleb was on his feet as Mark finished speaking. They knew where they had to head to meet with Don. "Let us know if that helps."

Adam searched the building to find Frank.

"Frank. We've got a major problem."

Frank turned from where he had been writing on a white board, seeing the almost panic on Adam's face.

"Adam? Darbi and Flynn?"

"That's correct. Don's had to leave their safe house. It's been found. And Darbi has been doing some research. She's come up with a name." Adam handed over the paperwork.

Frank nodded, knowing that Don and his team would do their utmost with God's help to keep the couple alive. He scanned through the paperwork, picking up the most important notes at a glance. He tapped the final sheet, his eyes thoughtful.

"She's spot on, Adam. This man? He's always been one who we have suspected of many crimes. Only no one could prove anything. Head off and research. I'm deep into the other end of it. We'll meet in a couple of hours, if that works, and compare notes." Frank watched as Adam nodded and then walked, no almost ran, to his office.

God, this is where it gets so dangerous for these two. We can only do so much to keep them safe. The rest is up to You and You alone.

He turned back to his work, reading through what he had discovered and then working to make it into a succinct summary. That was done well before he needed to meet with Adam. That time, he spent in prayer before rising to his feet and looking for the younger man.

"Adam? What have you come up with?" Frank seated himself, his eyes on Adam.

"This. Darbi's good. She knows her town."

"She does. Considering she was ten when she moved here, she learned it quickly. And I can guarantee that she wants her family about now. We need to work with Don to find a place where we can get them all together."

"Here? We could use one of the conference rooms."

"That would work. You go make arrangements. I'll talk to Don and then to her family. Paul and Sue need to be here as well." Frank sighed as he rose. He had been working a long day and felt fatigued. And the day was far from over.

"You need to rest, Frank." Adam's quiet voice stopped him in his tracks before he nodded and walked away. Adam stood and watched him, concern on his face before he walked to secure the use of the conference room.

Don nodded at Paul as he pulled to a stop. He had just spoken with Frank and then to Mark and Caleb.

"We're heading for the police detachment, people. Frank has made arrangements for us to be there. Darbi, your family will head there. The same for your uncle and aunt, Flynn. We want you all together for now. We'll meet there and then decide where to take you." He raised his phone again, reading the text message before responding to it.

"The police station? Really?" Darbi was angry and starting to become combatant. She was like her cousin, Chani, that way.

"Darbi, it's okay. We do what they want. Right now, we don't have much of a choice." Flynn tried to

calm her down, knowing that would be next to
impossible.

Chapter 35

Darbi spun as the door to the room opened and Brinn and Gareth entered. She was across the room and hugging her sister. She was almost in tears, having missed her greatly. Gareth wrapped the women in his arms and prayed for them. He then turned to Flynn, a hand out to shake Flynn's.

Darbi reached for her aunt and her cousins, hugging them and holding on a little bit longer. She had been so afraid for them. Ashlynn moved away, finding Frank watching them. She turned to study the men in the room, finding Abe and Murphy there. She frowned before her brow cleared.

Darbi moved among the men, finding Abe and staring at him. Abe stared back, no expression on his face. He knew what she was up to and wasn't about to budge. She was not under his care. Even if she had been, he still would not budge on what needed to be done.

"Abe? Where's Emma?"

"She's still at home. She's working on this but she has an urgent investigation in the works as well." Abe pointed to Don. "He's the one that you need to speak with." He could hear Murphy choking back laughter and felt close to that himself. Darbi had that look that said she was ready to argue with him.

"I have. He hasn't said anything. We know who it is. When will he be arrested?" Darbi was adamant that she was correct and felt that the man should just be arrested.

"We get that, Darbi." Murphy spoke up. "We know what Darci has said. Frank is aware of that and if that profile fits with who you said. It's not our place to do that."

"Again, I get that. I just want this over. It's taken enough of our lives. Do you know that?" She turned and stomped away, leaving grins on the men's faces.

Flynn had been watching, waiting to see who would win the argument. He shook his head at Abe before he moved after Darbi, stopping her by wrapping her in his arms.

"Flynn? When will this be over?" Darbi was highly frustrated and angry and also afraid.

"Soon, sweetheart. Right now, let's spend some time with our families. We all need that. You've missed out on that this week. They are waiting for you over at that table." He pointed with his chin.

"I know that they are. I'm just afraid to go near them."

"And by not going to them, whoever this is wins. He's keeping you from what is important to you. Your family."

Flynn watched as Darbi absorbed his words. He could see her thinking it through before she nodded. Determination coloured her face.

"You are correct, love. He has won. By keeping us on the run and in hiding, he's won. He's kept us from our families. No more of that. We live our lives, just like we have said all along. If it means that we ditch Don and Abe and even Richard, then we do that." Darbi didn't know that Don and Abe were standing near her, listening to her.

Flynn shared a look with the two men, seeing resignation and understanding on their faces. He nodded, moving Darbi away and to her aunt. He then returned to stand by the two men, assessing them and then searching the room.

"What do we do, Don, Abe? How do we bring this man out?"

"And why would you word it like that?" Don was not sure what Flynn was meaning.

"I mean that you can research and investigate all you want. He'll go into hiding, that's a given. We need to force him out into the open. And the only way to do that is to put us out there. And I know you don't want that." Flynn kept his eyes on Frank and Adam who stood in front of him.

"You're correct, Flynn." Adam sighed, knowing that he had not found the man. "He is in hiding. We have a number of addresses that we are searching."

"He'll be on a property that you don't know about. That's how they work." Flynn reached into a pocket, pulling out a folded paper. "Try these addresses. You have until tomorrow morning. If you don't have him in custody, then Darbi and I walk out of here. Our families go with us. We will put ourselves out there until he makes a move. Just pray that he doesn't kill one of us. And I can almost

———

guarantee you that he is not the one in charge. Someone else is."

Flynn walked away to find his uncle, standing beside him in silence.

Paul watched the men who he had left staring after him.

"Threaten them, Flynn?" At Flynn's nod, Paul sighed. "How long did you give them?"

"Until tomorrow morning. Then we walk out. And I know that you all will walk with us. It's dragged on long enough. We need to end this and end this in the next couple of days."

"And we will. Now that you have given them an ultimatum, let's make plans. I know that Abe and Don will work with us. Frank and Adam can't. They have to follow the investigation and all the proper legal moves. And I know that my crew will cover for us. The same for anyone else that we count as friends."

"That's a lot of people, Uncle Paul." Flynn nodded at Ronan and Gareth. "When do your friends arrive, Gareth and Ronan?"

"They're here already. The ones who worked undercover? They are working the streets, trying to find someone to speak with them. Evan thought he had a line on someone and would be in touch."

"Good. Can we work it to make it happen tomorrow?" Flynn was exhausted, barely able to keep his eyes open but he was determined to stay the course.

Darbi sat with the ladies, her head bowed as they prayed. They needed that, she acknowledged, but she wanted to be out there, on the hunt for whoever it was. That made her angry because she wanted them so badly that she could almost taste it. Darbi sighed, surrendering her anger to Go. She had to do that, she knew.

Brinn moved in on Darbi when their prayers finished, an arm around her sister. To think that they had both faced this type of thing was not how she had envisioned their lives.

"Darbi? Do you know who?"

Darbi nodded, looking around. She said a name, loud enough that all the ladies heard her. They looked askance at her before Ashlynn and Sue shared a look. They had often talked about that very man, wondering how he was able to stay in business. They had heard the rumours of the crime he was reported to be involved in

"Okay, so how do we do this?" Eilis moved her chair closer. She eyed Flynn. "He'll have given an ultimatum."

"He has. Tomorrow morning. We talked about this before we had to run. We want to flush this man out. Only it means putting everyone of us at risk."

"And do you think we won't agree?" Chani moved to hug her cousin. "Let's make plans and then talk to our guys. Abe and Don and their men will provide protection. Frank and Adam will continue their investigation. How do we do this?"

Chapter 36

The next morning, Flynn simply reached for Darbi's hand and walked from the conference room, heading for the street. Their families followed them. Abe and Don had headed out before dawn, to send their men throughout the downtown area. That was where the couple planned to head.

Darbi drew in a deep breath. *This was it,* she thought. *This is where we find the monster and draw him out. At least, that's how we're planning it. Only plans can change. We know that. Lord, go before us and lead us in this. Protect us. Protect our families. Protect those who are here for us.*

Flynn was praying as well. He knew that things could go wrong and go wrong badly and quickly. He had faith in Don and Abe. Only he didn't think that this would help. He could only pray that it would.

The couple walked the downtown streets, nodding at acquaintances and friends, feeling that they were repeating a walk that they had done not that long ago. Darbi's steps slowed, drawing Flynn to a stop. He stared down at her and then up. He flinched as he felt the weapon jab his side. This is not what was to have happened, he thought, before they were forced to walk forward. Darbi's hand was tight in his and he could feel the trembling in it. He didn't dare look around for the security that was with him. The crowds had moved in and prevented them from getting close to them.

Darbi drew in a deep breath. *This is it,* she thought. *This is where we disappear and are never seen again.* She paused as a hand on her arm tugged her into a ramshackle building and then through it to a waiting car. She gave a small cry as she was shoved onto the back seat and then Flynn landed beside her. She didn't dare look at the men.

Flynn, however, studied the men, a frown on his face. *No,* he thought, *these are not hired thugs, not as how we think of them. They've taken us for a reason. And I don't think that reason is to kill us.*

Abe and Don slid to a halt, their running footsteps having taken them through the crowds. They both spun in circles, searching for the couple.

"Where are they?" Abe turned as Micah ran towards him. "Micah?"

"They disappeared?" Micah held up his phone. "Darbi activated her bracelet. We can track them. They're heading for the edge of town."

"Okay, let's head out. Don?" Abe turned to him.

"You head that way. We'll look around here, just to see if there is anyone that the authorities might be interested in. Say, like that young man there." Don was across the street, the youth grasped by the arm. Don led him away, a wave at Abe as he did so.

"Okay, Micah. What didn't you say?"

"I got the impression that they were taken to protect them. I know one of the men who took them. He's not a criminal. Instead, he works as an assistant for a millionaire here in town."

"He does? That puts a wrinkle into it, doesn't it?" Abe headed for his vehicle, stopping to speak with Darbi's family. "Ashlynn, ladies. They disappeared but Micah here says they're safe."

"Safe? How can that be?" Ashlynn rubbed at her face. "Find them, Abe. Bring them home. We'll all be at my place. We'll continue to work this as we can."

Abe stood and watched the house closely. They couldn't get close to it. The grounds were too clear for them to attempt that. And he could see the security cameras around. They stayed back in the trees, praying that they were not seen.

Darbi stood watching the men closely. Something was off about all this, she decided. She turned to Flynn, finding him watching her. He shook his head, a signal not to fight the men. She sighed. What was going on?

The sound of a door opening in the distance and then footsteps heading their way sounded. They could hear the thump of a cane as it hit the floor.

"Darbi? Flynn? Have a seat." The man who had taken them pointed to seats. "You're not with the man after you. In fact, we need your help. We have just realized that in the last day and were unable to find you until this morning. Your body guards did a superb job of keeping you safe. If the crowd had not moved in, we would not have been able to bring you here."

"And you couldn't have just called and asked us?" Darbi snapped at him, her mouth dropping open as she saw the older man who appeared. "Dr. Donald? You're here?"

"I am, Darbi. I regret that we had to do this. And I know that Abe and his men are outside. We'll make sure that they know you are safe and provide refreshments for them. I need your help. You will understand when I explain, given your medical training. And Flynn, this will be an exclusive for you for your work as a reporter. Here, let us have some refreshments. Then, if I may, I would like to pray with you both. We need that protection only God can provide. The man after you is vicious and has no heart. To have you two alive after all this time has shown God has been watching over you."

Darbi raised her head, realizing that she was safe. That this man, a prominent surgeon in town, would indeed do everything that he could to protect them. That was obvious. She could sense Flynn's hesitation and felt the same. But they did owe him the opportunity to speak with them.

"Dr. Donald. You asked for our help. How can we provide that?" Flynn finally spoke, his arm going around Darbi and pulling her tight to him.

"Thank you for listening to me." Dr. Donald set down the cup and saucer he had been holding. "What I have to tell you has been something I have been aware of only for a short time and have had to investigate it. I have reached out to Frank on the force this morning. He was disturbed to say the least. I will explain what I can and how it involves you two. You were connected years ago by this man, without being aware of it. In fact, I could safely say that you would not have been aware of his interest in you.”

“Okay, so what is it?” Darbi leaned forward, a frown on her face. She was exhausted and the dark circles under her eyes and the whiteness of her face showed that.

“What is it?” Dr. Donald shared a look with his assistant. “What I am about to say is gruesome and horrible. Someone here in town has been killing people and harvesting their organs for sale.”

Darbi gave a choked cry before she turned her face into Flynn. His arms tightened on her as shock covered his own face.

“What? How can that be? And how do we fit in?” Flynn was very much puzzled.

“It is true. He is a monster, to say the least. And how do you fit in? Darbi, he thinks that somehow you heard something when you were in the office one day. And Flynn, he thinks that you heard about it out west and that is why you moved back here, so that you could investigate. We know that it’s not true. But we need to flush him out and bring him to justice. And unfortunately, it seems as if it has to be you two that do that.”

Chapter 37

To say Darbi was disturbed at the news was an understatement. She felt sick, more sick than she had ever felt. She knew Flynn wasn't much better. Dr. Donald had confirmed her suspicions. That made it even worse. She had not even aware of what the man had been involved in.

"Was he the one?" She turned from the window, her eyes on Dr. Donald. She knew his reputation. In fact, she had once thought that she would work for him, only that hadn't happened.

"The one? I'm not sure what you mean, Darbi." Dr. Donald shared a look with his assistant.

"The one who made us marry."

Dr. Donald drew in a sharp breath. She had just confirmed another suspicion of his. There had been rumours that had reached him, that this monster as Darbi called him had forced her and Flynn to marry.

"I believe so, Darbi. It is a rumour that I heard. We have reached out to the minister that was involved. He did confirm that he had married a couple. Only, he would not confirm names. He was terrified to say the least." Dr. Donald pointed to her seat. "Have a seat, Darbi. We've asked your friend, Abe, to come in and bring one of his men with him. They have been taken care of, provided with shelter and food as they have needed it. It has been a long day for you and it is not over yet. Not by a long shot as my father would have said. We need to make plans."

Abe and Murphy hesitated as they entered, not sure about what was really happening. They were happy to see Darbi and Flynn waiting for them. They just weren't sure about the others in the room.

"Abe. Murphy. This is Dr. Donald. He has news for you that is absolutely horrible." Darbi hid her face against Flynn, whose arms tightened around her even as sorrow crossed his face.

"Abe. Murphy. My apologies for how we made contact with these two. It was imperative that we get them away from that area and as soon as we could. I have reached out to the investigators and spoken with them. They were shocked at what I had to say but are agreeable for these two to stay here for now. No one is aware of where they are. Just you two."

"And Don and his team. They are working to keep the families safe. That is imperative." Abe refused to back down. His face was expressionless but Murphy could see the anger simmering underneath.

"That is fair. It is what is needed. As to what is going on with these two, the man who we are after did force them to marry. I have the name of the minister and spoke with him. He did not confirm that it was them, but the day and time that he was here matched that.

"As to why they were married, it is basically that man who forced it thought that they were cognizant of what he actual does. He is a butcher, to put it mildly. He murders people to harvest their organs. He has done that for years. It is only recently that we have been able to find the proof that we need in order to bring him to justice."

Abe and Murphy looked sick as they realized what the implications were. They shared a glance before glancing at Flynn. They could see that he was deeply troubled and they could understand why.

"Where do we come in?" Murphy finally found his voice.

"We would ask that you work with us to keep these two safe. My home is available for that. My wife has traveled out of the province with our daughter and grandchildren for a vacation. They are away until next week. But I don't think we need all that time. I understand that your wife, Abe, had found the information on this man."

Abe gave nothing away, a mask over his face.

"She may have. I don't always hear what her investigations are. How do we go about this? Don't you have to be out and about with your surgery?"

"No, not this week. I have booked these two weeks off. Knowing that my wife would be away, I planned to do some work around her to surprise her. I have put that off for now. This is much more important. We need to find this man and bring him to justice. Rumours that have reached me are that he is planning two more murders within the next day or so." His eyes tracked to Flynn and Darbi and then back to Abe.

Abe drew in a deep breath. He knew who would be the ones murdered and he would do everything possible to prevent it.

"Do you know where we can find him? I understand that he is in hiding."

"I do know. I have provided that information to the investigators. Unfortunately, he won't appear unless these two appear. And if they appear, it may mean their deaths." Dr. Donald looked over at the couple again, finding them asleep. "They need to sleep but we need to plan. That's where you come in, Abe and Murphy. We want to work with your team to do that. My men, while armed at times, are not in that line of work. I have one assistant and a driver. Please say that you will help."

Abe and Murphy stared at one another before Abe excused himself. He needed to make a phone call and needed privacy to do that.

"Emma? Hi." Abe heard Emma speaking with their son before she came back on the line. "What do you have to tell me?"

"Abe? Do you know where Flynn and Darbi are?"

"I do. I'm with them at the moment."

"Good. Now this is what I have. Do you know a Dr. Donald?"

"Why? I'm at his house."

"Oh no, this is worse than I thought. You need to get away from there and get them away. He's the one. I tried to get you, but I couldn't reach you."

Abe sighed. It was what he had expected. The doctor had been throwing them a line and he knew that Flynn and Darbi had believed him.

He turned as he heard footsteps. His six team mates stood there, stern looks on their faces.

"Abe? What is going on? I don't like the look on your face."

"And you'll like it even less when I tell you that the one who wants them dead is the one who has them in his house. We need to come up with a plan to get them away. Don't eat or drink anything."

"We haven't been. Micah had found this house as a suspect place just after you and Murphy went in. I reached out to Adam. He wasn't aware that we were here. He said he's working on search warrants and will be here shortly." Ian turned as he felt a hand on his shoulder.

Adam stood there, along with a number of officers.

"How many inside, Abe?" Adam kept his voice low.

"Three of them. Darbi. Flynn. And Murphy. I need to get back inside." Abe moved away, heading back inside, trusting that his team and Adam would come up with a plan to get them away.

"How do we do this, Adam? If it were just us, we'd move in." Micah was troubled.

Adam looked around, seeing the ETF members ready to move in. It was a decision that he didn't want to make but had to.

"Go ahead. You have more experience in this than we do. Our team will be ready to move in right behind you. Go with God, my friends."

Chapter 38

Abe returned to his seat, a slight nod given to Murphy. He turned his attention back to Dr. Donald, finding himself the attention of deep scrutiny. His face gave nothing away. His eyes shifted to Darbi and found her watching him through slitted eyes. She was trying her best to give the impression that she was still asleep. Abe next studied Flynn and deduced the same for him. He would need to make a move without Murphy being in on it. Only he figured Murphy had a good idea of what was going on.

"Okay, Dr. Donald. How do we do this? How do we keep these two safe? We'll need to move them somewhere else. You can bet that he's aware that you have them."

"I don't think so. They will be safe here. Your men will be here to watch out for them." Dr. Donald rose and walked away. His assistant stayed, his gaze intent on Abe and Murphy.

"Abe?" Murphy's voice was low.

"Sit tight, Murphy. We have a plan to get out of here."

"I thought so." Murphy rose, walking around, stretching as he did so. He had assessed the room and the risk when Abe had been outside. There was only the assistant in the room. Somehow they needed to take him down and then run with Darbi and Flynn. Only, he couldn't see how that would happen.

Dr. Donald returned, a tray in his hands.

"Help yourself, gentlemen. Just a slight refreshment for you." He had a gleam in his eyes that Abe didn't trust.

"Thank you, Dr. Donald, but we're fine for now. I need to walk through your house if I may, just to see where my men would be best positioned." Abe paused as he saw the gun appear in the doctor's hand. "Dr. Donald?"

"You're not going anywhere. Neither one of you. Sit down." He almost yelled at them.

Abe and Murphy sat again, only not together and not in the chairs that they had originally used. Murphy was very close to the assistant. Abe had chosen a chair just five feet from the doctor. They knew that a movement was needed soon. Murphy caught the soft sounds in the hallway and sighed. The others were now inside. That evened the odds to some extent. They still needed to take down the doctor and his assistant.

The chiming of the doctor's phone startled everyone. Dr. Donald pulled out his phone, listened and then tucked it away again. Abe's eyes narrowed before he sighed to himself. There was someone else, just as they had thought. It was a stand off at the moment. A movement in the hallway caught his eye as he glimpsed Joseph briefly. They would need to make a move soon and he was afraid for the couple with them. He began to pray for an avenue to get them away and take down the doctor and his assistant. *No, Abe thought, bodyguard. There is no way that is just an assistant. I have seen this too many times.*

Murphy stood and began to pace, drawing the ire of the doctor who commanded him to sit. His attention on Murphy, he didn't see the quick and quiet moves of Luke and Nathaniel as they reached in and quickly removed the bodyguard, a hand clapped over his mouth to still his cries. Abe was on the move, diving for the doctor, taking him down, hearing running footsteps coming to his aid. Others, including Murphy, had Flynn and Darbi on their feet and out of the door.

Darbi could hardly stop her sobs as Joseph's arm around her helped her run from the house. She could hear Flynn behind her. Adam reached for her as well, the two men almost carrying her away. Matt appeared, ready to assess them. He was the paramedic on the team and would know better than any of the others if they needed medical treatment

Darbi sobbed quietly, her emotions all over the place. Flynn simply sat beside her, an arm around her. He didn't care if Matt was muttering at him. His bride needed him and he would not let her go.

Adam headed for the house, hearing a shot, on the run. He slid to a halt on the hardwood floor, staring at Abe and his team and then down at the floor.

"Abe? What happened?"

"He managed to get away and get a gun. He killed himself." Abe rubbed at his forehead with a thumb and forefinger. This was not what the plan had been. The doctor had been stronger than they thought. "His cane was all a plant, a plan to make him seem feeble."

"That's likely true. We'll need your statements. The other two men?"

"They're tied up in the kitchen. We were able to do that." Ian stood back from the doctor, sorrow on his face. "Does this end for them?"

"No, it doesn't. He wasn't working on his own. There was someone behind him. We just found out that name. Now we have to find that person."

"A woman." Luke spoke up. "A woman who wanted it all and didn't care who she had killed in her desire to have it all." He nodded towards the outdoors. "They would have been next."

"That's what we have heard. Now, let's clear this out for the crime scene team and the coroner."

Abe walked towards Flynn and Darbi, his face dark with his thoughts. He paused as Matt approached him.

"Matt? Talk to me."

"I think that they were given something. Their movements and reactions suggest a sedative of some kind. I have assessed them but they need an official assessment for the record. What happened in there?"

"The good doctor killed himself. He's gone to face a higher judge."

Abe walked past Matt, feeling Matt's hand rest on his shoulder for a moment. They would meet later for prayer and to debrief, but for now, Darbi and Flynn still needed them.

Flynn opened his mouth to speak and then snapped it closed. It wasn't good, he could tell. His eyes moved past Abe to stare at the house. How could someone who had taken an oath turn so evil? Then he sighed. He had seen it before and in a friend's life.

Chapter 39

Adam watched the group as they had gathered in Flynn and Darbi's home. There was still a lot of work to do. They were closing in on the one responsible, a woman as had been guessed. They just couldn't find her. That meant Darbi and Flynn were still at risk. Adam didn't like that at all. He and Frank had talked. They wanted it over for the couple and over now.

Darbi approached him, a mug of coffee extended towards him.

"Thank you, Adam, for all that you have done. It is a relief to have some of those after us dealt with. But you are troubled still."

"I am, Darbi. And that means that you two aren't safe yet. We want this over for you."

"We know that you do." Flynn appeared, his arm around his bride. "God is in control. He knows why you have not yet found the woman."

"And who says it's a woman?" Adam grinned at him.

"It has to be." Darbi was adamant on that. "Only a woman could be this cruel. At least that's what I think." She excused herself as the doorbell rang. She opened it, surprise on her face. "Evelyn? You're here. I don't understand why."

"Can we talk, Darbi? I need to talk with you." Evelyn Landry, an older lady who worked in the transcription firm, stood there.

"Sure. Come in. We can talk in the kitchen, if that's all right. It's the only room that doesn't have someone in it at the moment." Darbi lead the way and then turned to Evelyn, a frown on her face. "What is it that you wanted?"

"Are you coming back to work soon, Darbi?" Evelyn refused to meet Darbi's eyes.

"I don't know. Flynn and I have talked about it but I haven't made a decision on that yet." Darbi's eyes narrowed. There was something off about the other woman that bothered her. She needed to get her out of her house and now. "Listen, can we talk later? I have family here and should be with them."

Evelyn's sudden move in raising her hand startled Darbi. She stared at the gun pointing at her.

"Evelyn? What is this? What are you doing?"

"I am ending this. It's been you all along, you know. You walked into that place. It was mine, you know. All my idea. No one knew it. You came in and were praised all the time. I didn't need that work. I have money that I will never use. So I need you to die."

Darbi watched her closely. Evelyn's finger was not on the trigger. Darbi's hand was extended to point towards the hallway. She could see Frank and Adam standing in the doorway, watching closely, ready to move in when they could.

"You don't want to do that, Evelyn. I know that you had all those people killed. You didn't do it yourself. Hand me the gun."

———

"No, you need to die. So does that husband of yours. You were always showing off when you were a kid."

Darbi stared at her. That was the exact opposite of what she had always done. Then, she remembered.

"Your daughter. She died when she was only eleven. She needed a new heart and didn't get one in time. Is that what started this all off? You were making money on her death?" Darbi struggled to hide her emotions.

"Yes, that's it exactly. Now, move to the backyard. We'll take this outside." She motioned with the weapon.

As soon as she had moved it away from pointing at Darbi, Adam moved in, his hand grasping hers and preventing her from finding the trigger and shooting someone. Frank simply moved in and moved Darbi out of there and to Flynn's arms.

This broke up the gathering. Their house was now a crime scene again. Flynn and Darbi stood outside, arms around one another.

"I'm tired of this, Flynn. Is this the end of it?"

"I believe so. Adam said he would make sure that it was. He's asked to meet with us all again in a couple of days.

Adam was as good as his word, finding them all on the following Sunday afternoon, relaxing at Ashlynn's. Ashlynn had simply given him a hug and then pointed to the living room.

Frank approached him, a quiet word spoken, before he nodded. *It was over,* he thought, *over for them.*

"All right, everyone, I can finally give what information that I have." Adam set his plate down. He looked around the room, meeting Paul's eyes. "Paul, can we pray first?"

"We can at that." Paul led them off in a time of prayer, knowing that God would be the one to heal and comfort them all.

"Adam? Why?" Darbi was still confused.

"It wasn't her daughter that needed the heart, Darbi. It had been her husband. He died when they had not been married too long, leaving her with a young daughter to raise. He had needed a liver but none could be found that was a match. We believe that she was responsible for killing her daughter and then selling organs, but we can't prove it. She had her daughter cremated. That would cover anything.

"She did set up a system where she would find people who were outcasts or alone and have them killed. Dr. Donald was the surgeon who worked with her. He had lost his license in the last few years but that didn't stop them. He had quite the surgical setup in his basement. I am glad that you two survived that.

"As to making you marry? We can't come up with an explanation for that. The minister didn't know. His family had been threatened as I am sure you all gathered. Evelyn Landry is refusing to say why the marriage. We think it was some sort of scheme to get back at one of you, but we don't know why. She refuses to say or to admit that she knew your parents, Flynn."

"God knows why." Darbi snuggled down against Flynn, happy that he was her groom. "Anything else?"

"No, that's about it. Dr. Donald is the one responsible for what all you two went through. He is also responsible for having Frank shot. He wanted him out of the way to get to you two. Only that didn't work out."

Adam listened to the happy voices around him. Frank watched Adam and then turned his attention to the Whitman ladies. Brinn and Gareth were settled and happy. Chani and her Ronan were planning their wedding in the near future. Darbi and Flynn had survived what they faced and were deeply in love. His attention stopped on Eilis and then Ashlynn. He prayed for them, knowing in his heart that they would be facing something. He just wished he could stop it. Only God was in control and not him.

Epilogue

Back from Chani and Ronan's wedding, Darbi ditched her shoes, finding the heels hard to walk in after a few hours. She was happy for her cousin. They made a cute couple, she thought. Flynn paused in the doorway, watching his bride. He loved her so much. He was just sad that they didn't have the memories of a day like this.

"Do you mind, sweetheart?"

Darbi turned to him, a frown on her face.

"I'm not sure what you mean." Darbi moved towards him and into his arms, reaching for his kiss.

"A day like today. You were robbed of it, sweetheart. You don't have those memories that you should have." Flynn watched as she shook her head

"I'm fine. Flynn, how about you?" Her head went against him as he shook his. "We are together. We are madly in love. What more could we need? I mean, it would have been wonderful to have had our families there. They missed out on that."

"It would have been nice." He turned her to the office, sitting on the couch there and drawing her down. He knew that she wanted to go and change out of her fancy outfit to something more comfortable. He loved her all dressed up and never failed to tell her that.

"I talked to Jonathan this morning when you were out running errands. He is so happy with your work. He wants to expand your columns."

———

"That's what he said. I told him that I had to discuss that with you and then pray about it."

"And we will." Darbi grew pensive. "I'm not sure what I want to do."

"Do research. That you are good at. I know Richard or Don would welcome you as part of their team, working behind the scenes."

"They have both said that. Garrett offered me a position as well. I just don't know."

"Don't rush into anything. We don't need the money from your work." Flynn stretched out his legs. "I like the colours that you are choosing. They were dated before."

"It was your parents' home. You hadn't had a chance to make it your own. Now, we are making it ours." Darbi's pensive look deepened. "Flynn, have you thought about a pet?"

"A pet? No, not really. I mean, if you want a cat or dog, that's fine with me. Why that question?"

Darbi shrugged, not sure on why she had asked that.

"I don't know. If God blesses us with children, I would like to see them with a pet. I miss my tabby but she was just so sick."

"We will do that." Flynn grew pensive in turn. "God blessed me with you. He protected us and led u through all this. He used us to stop other people from dying and by dying bringing sorrow to their families. We have also been able to help bring closure to those families whose loved ones were killed."

"He did. I was just so afraid that you would be killed. God did protect us. I didn't think of how much until I went back through it all the other day. Darci suggested that I write down my thoughts and feelings and I have been doing just that."

"I'm glad. Doug and Darci have become good friends."

They grew quiet, content in one another's company. Darbi rose at last, heading for the stairs and to change. She paused for a moment, thankfulness flooding her. God had provided just the man whom she needed and one who would lead their family in their walk with God.

Partway up the stairs, she paused and then headed back down them. She stood in the kitchen doorway, a soft smile on her face. She watched Flynn as he moved around, preparing his coffee, her tea, and a meal for them. He had ditched his suit jacket and tie, his shirt unbuttoned at the neck and the sleeves rolled up past hist elbows. A soft whistle sounded as he worked around the countertop, the song one of the ones that had played during the ceremony.

Darbi simply moved into his space, knowing that she would be welcomed. Flynn's arms caught his beloved bride close to him, reaching down to kiss her. They simply stood for a while, content to be with one another, their love evident for everyone to see.

Thank you for reaching out and picking up the story of Darbi and her Flynn, the third in the series. She was very open with their story and it was written in just a matter of days. I was off work on vacation, which was a good thing. The love that grew between them and the danger that they faced felt all too real at time. The reason for their danger? That was totally unplanned and unexpected. My characters love to do this to me, throw in curve balls and just allow me along for the ride.

As always, beloved characters walk in and out of the story. This time Darbi and Flynn drew in many. Abe and Emma and their team's story are in the *His Guardians* series. Frankie and his Deirdre are in *The Haven of Rest* series as are Gideon and Rebecca. Doug and Darci are in *The Heart of a Lion*. Dave and his Rylee's story is *A Touch of His Garment*. Jacob and his Finn are in the *Mistletoe Treasures* series. Don and Richard and their teams have not had their stories told but they are becoming very vocal about that. Evan and Tag's stories are part of *His Dreamseekers* series.

God has blessed me with a love of reading, something that I shared with my Mom. While writing this story, the fifth anniversary of receiving the very first copy of the very first novel I ever wrote passed. *The Sparrow*, part of the *Under His Wings* series started off my journey. Thank you to those who have been along for the ride, as my father would say.

The parable of the wise virgins has always been a favourite of mine. I can remember as a child hearing our pastor at the time preach a sermon on it. That has stuck with me. My father would often mention it. Dad was a carpenter but build furniture for me in his later years. He built me a stand for my keyboard, an organ stand that he called it. It has a high back with a music book rack, a roll top cover, storage on either end. I treasure it because it was something that he designed and created, a one of a kind piece. When he did it, he included some very precious things on it. On the back underneath the keyboard portion are seven pieces of wood. These he said were the seven churches in Revelations. On the top of the book rack, he carefully handcrafted what look like lamp chimneys. There are five. These he told me were the five wise virgins from the parable. Dad spent a lot of time in thought but never talked a lot about what he was discovering in Scripture. When he did, it was something like this. Dad graduated to heaven in 2012, about two and a half years after Mom. They are missed so very much.

Once more, thank you for being part of this journey that God has me on. I often set aside the keyboard, thinking that it is done, only to pick it up again as there is one more story that has to be told.

God bless each one of you. May He richly bless your life as you serve Him where He has placed you.

Ronna

www.ingramcontent.com/pod-product-compliance
Lightning Source LLC
Chambersburg PA
CBHW061255210726
48293CB00003B/973